ALSO BY ANN ARENSBERG

Sister Wolf

This is a Borzoi Book
published by Alfred A. Knopf

GROUP SEX

GROUP SEX

Ann Arensberg

ALFRED A. KNOPF   NEW YORK   1986

Library of Congress Cataloging-in-Publication Data

Arensberg, Ann [date]
Group sex.
I. Title.
PS3551.R398G7 1986   813'.54   86-45262
ISBN 0-394-55310-1

For Marie Brenner and Joanne Michaels

O, when shall Englishmen
With such acts fill a pen,
Or England breed again
　　Such a King Harry?

—Michael Drayton, *Agincourt*

I've been in this town so long
So long to the city
I'm fit with the stuff
To ride in the rough
And sunny down snuff I'm all right
By the heroes and villains.

—The Beach Boys, "Heroes and Villains"

Frances Girard lived in somebody else's house. "You have real-estate luck," said her friends when they first saw the narrow brick building attached to a row of houses on a tree-lined block. "It's not fair," said Edie Childs, who had come to visit; "you have a garden." Frances lived under the roof on the garret story. There were four floors in all, and three long flights of stairs to climb. "Heat rises," said Edie. "You'll be miserable in the summer." Frances had three large rooms, each with a marble fireplace and beaded moldings. The living-room furniture was covered in dusty-rose linen. The bedroom had a four-poster bed and a desk by the window. "A canopy? And curtains?" said Edie. "I hope you're not allergic to dust." Edie was unmoved by the Persian rugs and the mirrored sconces. She glanced at the claw-footed bathtub without a comment. She was absorbed in making a tally of the garret's drawbacks: the fourth floor was not walled off into separate quarters; there was no private entrance, only the central staircase; Frances walked through her landlady's house to get in or out. "You're not a real tenant, Frances; you're like a boarder." She inspected the doors that opened onto the landing. Sniffing with pleasure, she announced that they did not lock. "I have an idea," said Frances; "say something nice."

Frances and Edie had grown up in Cincinnati. They became best friends in grade school by a simple ritual. Edie walked up to Frances one recess and staked her claim: "Jody is moving to

3

Pittsburgh. You're my new best friend." Frances said, "Sure," since she had no other offer, and then they linked little fingers to seal the pact. Being best friends gave Edie certain rights. Frances never used her veto, if she knew she had one. Edie called every night to harmonize their costumes, to be sure they wore matching sweaters or matching socks. Edie saved Frances a seat on the bus or in the classroom. They shared their lunches when Frances brought a roast-beef sandwich. Edie attached herself to Frances at dancing classes. She was so fearful of sitting out dances that she made Frances turn away partners until she had been chosen. By the time Edie had been asked, all the boys were dancing, so it was Frances who waited alone on the row of gilt chairs. Edie had married Hilliard P. Childs when she was only twenty, to avoid the unthinkable prospect of sitting out life. Now that Edie was the wife of a New York City lawyer, she shared her matronly wisdom with her spinster friend. Frances did not always take her advice in a generous spirit. She was apt to turn sly and sulky and dodge her questions. A little evasiveness never discouraged Edie. She had Frances's welfare in mind, so she stood her ground.

While Edie examined the bathroom, which had no towel-rack, Frances slipped away to her kitchen to make some tea. When Edie came in, she found Frances on a stepladder, fumbling through cans and boxes on the upper shelf. Edie addressed her, but Frances appeared not to hear. Edie sat down and started to have her say.

"I'll make you a bet. It's going to end in tears. You're already watering her plants and sorting the mail."

The kettle was whistling. A can of tomatoes fell down and dented the counter. The can rolled off the counter and onto the floor, striking the legs of the ladder as it tumbled, making a racket, but not enough noise to hush Edie.

"She knocked on your door when you were reading. You put

on your robe and went down to sit by her bedside. You stayed up till two when she was ready to go to sleep. Did you bring her a hot-water bottle and tuck her in?"

"She has terrible insomnia," said Frances, filling the teapot.

"You don't," said Edie. "If you don't get nine hours, you're apt to turn mean and cranky."

Frances filled the teapot too full. Water splashed on the stove and hissed on the electric coils.

"You're not like a tenant, Frances; you're like a paid companion."

"She watered my plants last weekend. Plus she answered my phone."

"Hnff," said Edie as Frances spooned out tea leaves. "I want mine weak."

Frances set the cups and teapot on the table. "Pour it when you think it's ready. You haven't met her."

"I don't have to meet her," Edie said; "it would warp my judgment."

Frances snorted with laughter. Self-awareness from Edie always won her back. When Edie was acting like the barbarian hordes, mowing down all resistance to her notions, Frances dug farther and farther down her mole hole. When Edie made fun of her Hunnish alter ego, Frances scurried out and followed her where she led. There were two Edies: one meant well, and one meant mischief, and Frances was not always able to sort them out. Frances wanted some of Edie's gumption and Edie's malice, but when she borrowed them, she often found they did not fit. At the moment, she felt like playing by Edie's rules, so she threw her a meaty bone to worry clean.

"Just a second. You have too met her. Two years ago, at Mother's eggnog. On Christmas Day."

"I remember your ma put green crème de menthe in the eggnog."

"That wasn't Mother. That was Mother's second husband."

"It wasn't Henry's idea to wrap brandied cherries in bacon."

"Madeline was there," said Frances. "I know you met her. Weed Bissell brought her. You must remember him."

"Not fondly," said Edie. "I thought her name was Burdick."

"She dropped Weed and married George Burdick. They lasted six months."

"That should teach her to steer clear of men whose names start with B."

"George was a villain. Poor Madeline. She told me she thinks that life has passed her by."

"Just a lonely grass widow, devoted to worthy causes."

"The orphans loved her. They came here last Sunday for supper. She read them stories. They never misbehaved."

"Of course not. They're biding their time. The first sound you hear will be Madeline's dying shriek."

"Don't be a pit viper, Edie. They were six-year-olds."

Had Edie stamped her foot beneath the table, or had Frances heard the radiator knocking? A purple flush spread over Edie's cheekbones. The radiator showed no change in color.

"You stop it, Frances. That's a wormy trick." She bipped the table with her open palm. "You make me say bad things when you're too scared to."

"I like Madeline."

"You're just saying so to spite me."

"Why do you have to have opinions about my friends?"

"That's what you need me for. To have opinions."

"Will you let me like her, please? I have to live here."

"The only thing you have to do is pay the rent."

Up the stairwell drifted a medley of new sounds: a thud, like a closing door; a creak of footsteps; several voices, growing louder, then receding.

"Oh, blank," said Edie. "I'll have to deal with Madeline. I'm never coming back unless she's out."

Frances felt too embattled to demur. "We'll get your coat. I put it in the closet."

Frances led the way and opened the closet. The light went on. Edie elbowed her aside. She yanked down a dress that had been thrown over the clothes rack.

"This is new," she charged. "You're always keeping secrets."

Edie riffled through a group of garments hung on hangers, tearing the cleaner's plastic with greedy fingers.

"Evening pajamas? Taffeta with flounces? I must say, Frances, they don't look much like you."

"Madeline was cleaning out her closets. The rest of them went to cancer and mental health."

"How nice for them. Do her clothes have healing properties?"

"Can it, Edie. Would you kindly keep your voice down?"

"Is she paying to have these lovely cast-offs altered? They'll be too small. She wants you to feel fat."

Edie could go on stinging like a swarm of bees, and Frances had never perfected an antivenom. The barbs raised welts, but the stings were well deserved. Frances had whetted Edie's appetite for aspersion, and served up Madeline on a garnished platter. Edie had grabbed the bait, but Frances had salted it. For that matter, Edie did not need a lure. All the actors in Frances's life were Edie's prey. She did not have to know them in order to make a meal of them, as long as she could gnaw on a single toothsome detail. Frances had mentioned that Ruthanne Marvin, her secretary at the Harwood Press, wrote fine reports and had a talent for editing. "Get rid of her," Edie had said. "She wants your job."

Frances found Edie's coat and shut the closet. The door was

hinge-bound, so she could not make it slam.

"You don't want me to have other friends. That's how it sounds."

"I don't mind," said Edie, kissing her goodbye. "What I mind is that I'm not allowed to pick them."

Frances was holed up in her office behind closed doors. Panda Wattel (who pronounced her name "Wattelle") had come in to have a conference about her manuscript. The working title of her novel was "AfterBirth" (one word, with a capital A and a capital B). Frances had never inquired how Panda got her own first name, for fear it was because she was overweight and round-eyed. Panda Wattel was Mr. Harwood's only niece, and Mr. Harwood had quickly palmed her off on Frances, the youngest editor and least likely to rebel. Albion Harwood, the president and founder, was only fifty, but his hair was white. His pale gray eyes seemed fixed already on eternity. He loved books but lived in dread of those who wrote them, since authors, not to mention authoresses, were walking vessels of petty grievance and conceit. Authors never perceived, as painters were obliged to, that once a work was finished it passed beyond their reach, like a child who has grown up and left the nest. Mr. Harwood had built a bathroom in his office, not because he was modest or undemocratic but in order to vanish during an author crisis. According to the friendly office wag, Mr. Harwood could hear an author demanding more advertising from one end of the corridor to another, even if the demand was made over the telephone.

In the case of Panda Wattel, or Wattelle, Mr. Harwood was right to expect an author crisis. Besides being his only sister's only daughter, Panda claimed to have been the favorite student of Philip Roth during one of that famous writer's teaching stints at a Boston program for adult education. Mr. Harwood had not read his niece's novel, though he had picked it up and ruffled through the pages. Frances had told him that it was a "woman's book," and a strange expression had darkened his kindly visage, as if he were a guest at the table of an Afghan chieftain and had been presented with a special dish of roasted sheep's eyes. Like her book, Panda filled her uncle with disquiet. He did not want to be kissed in front of the receptionist, nor hallooed at from his doorway during meetings. History does not record his feelings on those occasions when he discovered her hairbrush in his private bathroom. Early this morning, Frances had found him in his office pointing a ruler at the center of the rug, as if he had been measuring the area to cut out a trapdoor. Before she could manage to capture his attention, he walked over to the bank of windows and looked down. Poor Mr. Harwood. There was no exit through the windows. The Harwood Press was on the twenty-seventh floor.

Frances shared her employer's visions of quick escape. Her own office had turned into Panda's pied-à-terre. Panda had left behind, or stashed for her convenience, a portable typewriter, an overnight case, and a raincoat, as well as three shopping bags full of outlines and revisions. There was another suitcase full of notes on cards, and typed biographies of all the characters in her book. Panda felt that any novelist worth her laurels should know everything about the people she imagined, including family trees as far back as Columbus, although most of these facts were left out of the plot. It was no wonder that "AfterBirth," in its first version, had weighed in at nine hundred pages, with no margins.

Frances and Panda were working on the love scene (the love scene with *penetratio,* not the clothed one), which explained the

PLEASE KNOCK sign taped on Frances's door. Before the meeting, Panda had unrolled a giant chart and tacked it up over Frances's favorite book-fair posters. The chart demonstrated that episodes in the novel were synchronous with important world events. Thus the big love scene (in which the heroine inserts her diaphragm) took place while Dr. Barnard performed his first heart transplant, and the clothed love scene (which happened in a toolshed) coincided with the death of Boris Karloff.

Frances peered at the chart for several tactful minutes. Panda read her silence as all-consuming interest.

"That's how I work," she said, with a little laugh. "My characters stand for something larger than themselves."

Panda's characters certainly had a monstrous aspect, but that was not Dr. Barnard's fault, or Mr. Karloff's.

Frances geared herself up to ask the fatal question. "Are you saying you want the chart put in the book?"

"Oh, no," said Panda, casting her round eyes downward as if Frances were paying her an undue honor. "Don't you think it would overload the average reader?"

"I'm with you there. Let's spare the average reader." Frances hoped her relief did not show on her face.

"Could we get to work?" Panda liked to be in charge. She flipped through her manuscript and found some marked-up pages. The marks were Frances's and Panda was frowning at them. Frances noticed a little pile of yellow thumbtacks that Panda had spilled and left underneath the chart. No doubt she assumed that the maid would pick them up. Her editorial maid-of-all-work had cleaned up her prose, but her frown implied that she thought the job was faulty.

Panda handed a page to Frances, then pulled it back. "Why won't you let me say 'Their need-ends met'?"

Frances tried to invoke the spirit of Philip Roth. How had

that phrase slipped past His caustic eye? She captured the page, but it took a little tugging. She found the sentence in question and read it slowly, moving her lips as if the words were foreign. Then she read it out loud, enunciating clearly.

"'Their need-ends met, and they entered The World Apart.'"

When she looked up, Panda was smiling a far-off smile, entranced by her choice of imagery and language.

"Panda?" Frances broke the spell. "Tell me. What are 'need-ends'?"

Panda reached for the page, as if to refresh her memory. She held it up close; then she held it at arm's length.

"'Need' is need," said Frances, "but what are 'ends'? Is that 'ends' as in 'means to an end,' or nether parts?"

"They're in bed," said Panda.

"I gathered that," said Frances. "And while we're at it, where is The World Apart? Is it on a map? It's spelled with capital letters."

Panda pressed the page to her bosom like a shield. "Mr. Roth never raped my work. I got an A."

Mr. Roth had never raped Panda in any sense, which probably inflamed her present sense of injustice. Frances decided to retreat and fight another day. She did not want to sneer at Panda or hurt her feelings. She did not want to hear Panda's lecture about the artist, that lonely pilot soaring above the herd, dropping cargoes of hope and meaning to upraised fingers. Art, with its letters scrambled, came out "rat," a fact that Panda would be advised to ponder. Even less did she want to hear her views on sex, a gagging brew of smegma, sperm, and spirit ("spirit" as in "soul," not alcoholic content). Frances thought about her newest writer, Gloria Cohen, whose book was almost ready for the printer. Gloria would never put viscid juices in her stories, or rods or shafts, or tender ripening buds, or pubic hair likened to a bunch of grapes, unless she wished to play a scene for humor.

For the rest of the day they worked on smaller issues, like Panda's habit of ending a sentence with a series of dots. Frances was saving her thunder for tomorrow's session, which would probably end in tense, high-pitched debate. She was ready to bargain if Panda stood her ground; she would trade her "The World Apart" for one stunning sentence: "Her breasts were as pink and ripe as sweet summer fish." The critics would have a field day with those fish. Why didn't Frances throw Panda, fish first, to the critics? She could not expose good Mr. Harwood to their spite, and besides Panda worked very hard, which compelled respect. In the course of a year she had written a thousand pages. Whatever might be the content of those pages, she had sat down and built a towering pile of paper. Frances had never committed herself to such a task. She had never risked public scorn or adverse judgment. Panda wrote so hard that she was forced to eat in restaurants. One day, while she was planning the opening chapter, she had taken a roast of meat out of the freezer, but the thought of it thawing and breathing on the counter had preyed on her mind and destroyed her concentration. Frances wondered if she would have been as much afflicted by a smaller item, like a package of frozen carrots. Because she was a writer, she was more sensitive than Frances. She lived in horror of foods with seeds, like squash or melons, and always cracked eggs with two bowls at the ready in case she opened an egg and found a blood spot. One day—not a working day—she had made a milkshake, putting milk and strawberries into an electric blender. When she saw the black specks floating in the mixture, she had swooned with fright and passed out on the floor. Creative people paid a heavy price, and Frances had put herself in the service of such people. Perhaps she had done so because she wished to be more like them, although she knew she belonged to another, lesser species, the race of people who answer their phones and fold the bath towels, who never prowl the city streets at midnight, and who are not allowed to have a nervous breakdown.

Carrying a manuscript that had burst the clasp on its manila envelope, and a bag containing a leaky carton of milk, Frances put her key in the lock of Madeline's front door and tried to turn it without making any noise. Inside the door she stood very still and sent out radar. The kitchen was empty and the doors to the garden were closed. There was no handbag on the table in the vestibule, but the door on the parlor-floor landing was halfway open. Frances started to climb the steps, keeping close to the wall because the sections next to the railing were apt to creak. She walked in a zigzag course across the landing; she knew the strengths and weaknesses of every floorboard. She reached the second floor, which was Madeline's quarters, her bedroom, dressing room, bath, and little study. Each door was shut and each room was an ambush from which Frances could be snared and then detained for hours. From behind a door would come that honeyed hoot, and Madeline would emerge with breathy, pressing business: the menu for an after-theatre supper; a plan for storing her mother's English china (green tags for Derby, red for Bow, and blue for Worcester). Did Frances want the maid to do her room? Would she like some ivy cuttings from the garden? The florist was coming, or the seamstress, or the cleaner, or the man in the funny top hat who swept the chimneys. Madeline had an appointment. Would Frances answer the doorbell? And make sure to show them out and bolt the door? Madeline was very busy, busier than Frances, who plodded to work at nine, then home at six. Frances had heard her express a wistful kind of envy: "How I wish I could take a lovely steady job; it would be heaven just to relax and follow orders!" Madeline handled more crises than a forest ranger in a drought, or maybe her description of small events was hyperbolic. Her natural style was the opposite of terse and factual: "I was up till nearly dawn with my accountant." "The windowsills are covered with a foot of filth." There was a good deal of make-work in Madeline's schedule. There was even more make-others-work. She lived by an unswerving private maxim: The simpler the task, the more hands are needed to perform it. Frances had often seen Madeline marching through the house followed by a train of minions and recruits—the maid, a neighbor's child, the window washer (anyone within her beck and call)—on her way to put new fuses in the fuse box, or to attach the sprinkler to the garden hose. Frances had brought up the rear in many of these processions, and had observed that the time required to finish a given task increased in proportion to the number of helpers who had been enlisted.

Frances reached the third floor without surprise or incident. It was safe to assume there was nobody in the house. The third floor, which contained two empty guest rooms, lay like a moat or trench between Frances's castle and the rest of Madeline's household—a dry moat and shallow trench, however, easy to ford and attractive to invaders. Madeline thought nothing of climbing two or three flights to have her dress zipped, or to ask Frances to open a jar with a stubborn lid. Her female guests had quickly picked up Madeline's habit. They saw Frances's apartment as an all-night drugstore or notions counter, where they could get aspirins, hand lotion, needles and thread, or buttons.

As she passed the open door of the second bedroom, Frances saw an object lying on the floor. There was a lot of Mrs. Tittlemouse in Frances, who picked threads off the carpet in the lobbies of grand hotels. She seized the object and held it up between thumb and forefinger. It was a necktie, which implied the presence of a man. If he had removed his tie, what else had he taken off? Was he still lurking, Pan-like, behind the full-length curtains? Frances inspected their hems; she saw no naked feet. The necktie was narrow and its label read Big Guy Menswear. Did Madeline have a blue-collar lover, and a large one at that? Would he leave sweat stains on her eyelet baby pillows and pick his teeth with the pasteboard corners of her monogrammed matchbooks? Would he break her spirit and make away with her unearned money? Would she lock herself in her room when he finally jilted her, leaving Frances to come and go in perfect freedom? At the thought of Madeline silent and invisible, Frances ran up the last flight of stairs with a gleeful heart.

Frances Girard kept a diary in a schoolchild's copybook. The diary lived in the drawer of her bedside table. It was entirely covered by a red bandanna folded to overlap the edges of the book by half an inch. On top of the red one was a blue bandanna, folded smaller, and on top of that a pile of paper tissues. The drawer also contained a jar of camphor chest rub, a nasal inhaler, a box of menthol cough drops, and a stick of salve for cracked or chapping lips. Anyone who opened the drawer would conclude that she had a cold, or was preparing for one, and would probably search no further.

Frances used her diary for the sake of mental hygiene, to record bad feelings and to leech them off, or to rewrite a dialogue in which she had been worsted, so that trenchant retorts, undelivered because of cowardice, would not reverberate in her mind for weeks on end. After a day that had contained a two-hour session with Panda, a telephone call from Madeline during a sales meeting, and lunch with Edie, who gave her a list of real-estate agents, Frances felt a need for the fellowship of her diary, which asked no favors and liked her the way she was. She sharpened a pencil and opened the drawer, then drew it wider. She pulled out the drawer and put it on the bed. The tissues on top of the kerchiefs on top of the copybook were crumpled and piled up too far to the left. The lip salve was upside down, the cough drops were spilled, and the inhaler had rolled underneath the red bandanna. She prayed to St. Francis de Sales, who protected editors, that Madeline was not the snooper and tissue-crumpler.

But who among her nearest or dearest was a better candidate? Was there anything nice about anybody in her diary? It was a wonder the notebook was not parched or charred from the venom and bile that Frances had spilled on its pages. If she wanted to do an analysis by the numbers, she would have counted more stones thrown at women than at men. Like the scholar who tallied the negative adjectives in *Moby Dick* and proved that Melville was a pessimistic author, Frances could have added up the carping references to her sisters and been forced to infer that she did not love her sex. Heading the list of female traits, and most repeated, were "slippery," "controlling," "erratic," and "underhanded," followed by "sidewinding," "needy," "entitled," and "unconscious." If women were slandered, so was their brand of friendship. *April 17, 1970: "I wish that my ears came off; then I could hand one to Sloan and get on with my business."* (Sloan Paddock had gone to work in San Francisco, but her rambling letters brought her back alive: "I am growing within as a woman . . . my energy is good . . . I feel centered when I'm wearing yellow . . . P.S. How are you?") *August 4, 1971: "I am a slop pail for unsolved problems. Or a coin machine. They put in their nickels and I say the right soothing things." January 31, 1972: "What can you expect of a sex with a hole in the center? Marla the astrologer told Panda that the feminine side was drowning in itself in her chart. Women are like stagnant pond life. The symbols for women are wet or dark or blind. I will never EVER 'keep track' of my period. (Panda circles the Date of Onset in* red pencil.)" *February 4, 1972: "Girls are deeply wormy but I do not worship boys. HOWEVER: boys do not serve up their troubles to chance acquaintances."*

The snooper, if there was a snooper, might have been appeased by the fact that Frances disliked her baneful thoughts. *March 26, 1972: "Speaking of worm life, who is the lowliest worm? I don't have to live on my belly. I could try standing on my hind legs." April 28th: "I get stepped on because I lie down in their path. Something about the worm attracts the foot." May 3rd: "Female friendship is like the Tunnel of Love in the amusement park. Creepy spidery wisps reach out suddenly and brush your face. Well, I was the one who picked them. Or did they pick me? It doesn't matter, since I haven't bolted. I've just stayed picked."*

Frances lifted the drawer and slid it back into the table. She remembered that her cover was blown and opened it again. She pulled out the diary and looked around the room. Should she hide it under the mattress or behind the bookshelves? Should she drop it in the garbage with the eggshells and empty bottles? Instead she decided to leave it on her desk, not only in plain sight but lying open, with a sharpened pencil protruding from the binding, ready to write the latest entry, May 13th.

Before she could exult in the rashness of her action, Frances heard a little scratching at the door, and a tiny, high-pitched sound, a mouselike bleat. Perhaps there was an animal in the corridor. She hoped it was not hurt enough to bite her. She opened the door and stepped back in surprise. It was two-footed, although it slumped and drooped, and tucked its tiny head against its shoulder. It resembled a wounded bird blown down the chimney, but it wore a robe tied slackly at the waist.

"Frances," said Madeline. "Will you rub my feet?"

Frances wondered if she should guide her by the elbow, but Madeline tottered toward the bedroom chair, sank back in a kind of swoon against the cushions, and raised her legs to rest upon the hassock. What Madeline was this, so altered and transported? Where was her jaunty stride, her bold halloo? This waif with the starving eyes was like her shadow, or the ghost of a Madeline called to an early grave. She needed a blood transfusion, not a foot rub. She needed a dish of spinach and raw liver. Frances watched her like an anthropologist who is new to fieldwork. Frances was a serious student of feminine wiles. She suspected that she might be in the presence of a little-known, uncatalogued example. She sat down on the far end of the hassock and hoisted Madeline's dainty hooves onto her lap.

"You look awfully funny, Madeline. Are you sick?"

"Oh, please," said Madeline. "Can't you rub with lotion?"

Frances got up to do as she was bidden, dropping Madeline's feet instead of easing them aside. She went into the bathroom and returned, carrying a hand towel and a bottle of Almond Balm. She spread the towel across her lap and went to work.

"Not the tips of the toes," said Madeline. "My nose stuffs up."

Frances began to rub firmly, both feet at a time, first the spots on the balls of the feet that correspond to the throat, eyes, back of the head, ears, lungs, and shoulders. She massaged the insides of the feet, which relate to the spine; then the centers of the feet, which soothes the larger organs; and, last, the edge of the heels, to relax the thighs. Madeline folded her arms across her chest like a corpse in a coffin, but she made little signs of life, chirps, sighs, and mews, sounds the rubbee makes to urge the rubber on in case she is tiring and feels inclined to quit.

"I am not such an evil person," Frances was thinking as she creamed and rubbed, stroked, kneaded, pressed, and chafed. "I may be a worm but I'm not a grudging worm. Rubbing Madeline's feet is a purely generous action. I am not deterred by grime nor scurf nor bunions, nor baby toes so small they look deformed. I do not have to love the owner of these feet, nor any other feet I have in hand. I do not want compensation for my rubbing. I do not want to borrow Madeline's ermine coat. I do not expect to be rubbed in return. I should know by now they never do rub back."

Always a rubber, that was Frances's lot: always a rubber, never a rubbee. Legions of feet had passed between her palms, mostly female feet; men's feet were tense and ticklish. She had found a Zone Therapy chart in the college bookstore. She practiced on her roommate and then on the girls next door. Her rubs became famous. The word spread from house to house. In the living room (when the housemother was not looking), girls would draw up their chairs and plop their feet into her lap. Some of these feet were savory and some were nasty; many were stockinged, but most of them were naked. Shapely feet waited their turn along with calloused.

Frances liked rubbing as well as any hobby. It gave her a role to play in that small community, like head of the dorm, or fire chief, or editor of the *Yearbook*. Rubbing feet gave her a protective cover; if everyone knew what she did, they would not try to guess who she was. No one asked her personal questions while she was rubbing; no one found out the names of her beaus, or what her grades were. She did not have to own her failures or disclaim her triumphs. As long as she rubbed, she was sure to be left alone.

She was left alone, but she had no time for herself. No one wanted her soul, but they did want the use of her hands. Frances was very busy. She posted her office hours on her dormitory

door. Every evening the line of clients stretched down the hallway. Frances would not take payment for her service, although
some girls had offered her serious sums of cash. In an effort to
reward her, her clients made excessive claims. Jeanne-Marie,
who came from Lyons, said the rubs cured her liver; Teresa,
from Nicaragua, swore the rubs helped her sleep. Patty ("Kel-
ler") O'Malley passed the word that she had thrown away her
glasses. Frances was besieged. Her room, or wherever she sat,
became Lourdes or Loreto, though no carvings of miniature
limbs were hung over her door. Roxy Grainger, who was failing
Czarist Russia, tracked Frances to her cubicle in the stacks and
begged her to rub the point that improved the memory. Annah
Lehr woke Frances at 4 a.m. imploring, "Where is the point to
fix a broken heart?"

Two squirming feet roused Frances from reflection, remind-
ing her that she had been neglectful.

"Do the heart point, Frances," said Madeline, in a whisper.

"What's wrong with your heart?" asked Frances. "Do you
need a doctor?"

"I should call a surgeon. I need my heart cut out."

Frances narrowed her eyes and rubbed the pituitary point.
She knew from experience that this point made Madeline jump.

"I get it. I'm slow tonight. You mean heart as in Cupid."

"It's not nice to laugh at me, Frances. I'm losing blood."

Frances eyed Madeline closely. Her chin was trembling. Her
porcelain teeth were biting her lower lip. What was happening,
anguish or bad theatre? With Madeline, it was difficult to tell.
Perhaps she was priming Frances to run romantic errands,
which would be more fun than watering Madeline's plants.

"Who's draining your blood?" asked Frances, priming back.

"He's famous," said Madeline. "You'd recognize his name."

"Just give me a hint. U Thant? Truman Capote?"

"Swear you won't tell. Could you rub the Achilles tendon?"

"Who would I tell? Is he married?"

"He lives with someone."

Frances was overjoyed. She had struck oil. She rubbed very fast so the gush would not dry up.

"Don't tickle," said Madeline. "She's an actress in his company."

"What company?" Frances asked. "The People's Mime Troupe? The Performing Drugstore? The Theatre In Your Head?"

"Did you see *Peer Gynt* on stilts at Hadley Airport?"

"Paul Treat!" said Frances. "I didn't see *Peer Gynt*. But I saw *As You Like It* with seals in Central Park."

"He keeps me waiting," said Madeline. Her feet were rigid. "He says he'll come and then he doesn't call. Sometimes he calls and then he doesn't come."

Frances cast a wary glance at Madeline. Her eyes were glazed and her voice had no inflection. If she were the heroine of a science-fiction movie, there would be a pea pod from outer space down in the basement sucking her will and making her a zombie. In his newspaper photos Paul Treat looked large and human, but perhaps all directors were kin to zombie-masters.

Madeline made a weak attempt to rise. Holding Frances's arm, she wobbled to her feet. She could stand by herself, but she could not stand up straight. Love, or infatuation, had cracked her backbone, which had been bent through the years by access to a trust fund.

"Go get some sleep," said Frances. "Take an aspirin."

Madeline heard nothing but the sound of her own thoughts. "I put money in his play. You'd think he'd be on time."

"Maybe he's a cad and a rotter," offered Frances.

"I bought ten shares. I should have taken fifty."

Madeline shuffled out the door and down the staircase, looking feebler than she had when she came in. Frances decided this case had been one of her failures. Unrequited love cannot be cured by foot rubs.

Frances woke up next morning feeling poorly. She sneezed a volley of sneezes and started coughing. She got halfway out of bed, then fell back down. Her limbs did not want the job of standing upright. Sometimes during a rub, if she did not keep her guard up, poisons passed through the rubbee's feet into her system, afflicting her with a kind of shadow illness. If that were the fact, then Madeline had waked up perky, leaving noble dog Frances riddled with her symptoms. Even now, as Frances tossed on her bed of pain, Madeline would be giving orders and writing checks. Perhaps she would pension off Paul Treat's actress and usurp her place, or bribe Paul Treat to come and live with her. A man in the house might share some of Frances's duties. Men were better at swiping cobwebs in high corners, moving heavy furniture, and coiling garden hoses. Unfortunately, men were apt to draw the line at rubbing feet and running household errands.

When had she turned from a tenant into a houseguest? When had she decided she was under obligation to straighten the bedspread on the way past Madeline's bedroom, or clean spots off the entrance-hall tiles with a moistened tissue? Or to barrel down two flights of stairs when she heard the telephone, so that Madeline would not miss a vital message? Was it kindness or fear that prompted these secret favors? Was Frances atoning for her own bad nature? Or for the fact that she had no sympathy for Madeline? "I don't like her," thought Frances. "I have to leave her house. I will find a little box in a boxlike building, with a door that locks, and a chain, and a one-way peephole."

At ten o'clock Frances ventured out of bed. She had slept off Madeline's glooms and got up hungry. She called Ruthanne to say she would be absent, then put on a robe and went into the kitchen. There were three sprouting onions and a jar of chutney in the icebox. The cupboards were crowded with items like beans and macaroni. Frances marched to the head of the stairs and cocked her ears. She listened long enough to make sure the house was empty. Egged on by her newfound spirit of rebellion, she set off to make a raid on Madeline's larder.

She was stopped on the third-floor stairs by a grinding noise, a sound produced by old or rusty plumbing. Row-house acoustics were often very tricky, so the faucet in use might be in the house next door. Frances briefly considered breakfasting on chutney; then she resumed her quest for plainer food. On the second-floor landing she tripped on the hem of her robe. She bent over to see if her toe had torn the stitching. Her sash became untied and fell away. As she grabbed for the sash, she saw two naked legs. She let her eyes rove very slowly upward. The naked legs sustained an outsized man. Clutching her robe and trying to tie the sash, she was caught at an unwelcome disadvantage, though no more so than the man in the bathroom doorway, who wore only a towel to hide his pride and shame.

Several courses of action seemed pertinent to Frances: run upstairs and hide in the closet; run downstairs and into the street; pull off his towel and throw it out the window; ask if he liked his fried eggs up or over easy. To her own surprise, and the big man's consternation, she sat down on the bottom stair and hugged her knees. She felt like a camera buff on a bloodless safari who has spied a lion dozing in the sun, close enough to watch his whiskers twitching, but not too close to hazard being

eaten. This fine mammal had a massive chest and sloping shoulders, and dead-white skin like the paintings of Spanish hermit
saints. The fur on his chest and legs was thin and black, but the
fur on his head and chin was thick and russet. She counted three
knowledge bumps on his vast, high brow. His startled eyes were
blue clouded with gray. His feet were flat but his toes were long
and slim, and the second toes were longer than the others. His
small hands, which were out of scale, clutched at the towel. The
beast seemed bewitched by Frances's close inspection; in that
state he could have been netted or roped at will.

Frances was much too curious to prolong the silence. She rose
to her feet and knotted her bathrobe sash. He stepped sideways
(a smaller person would have skittered), but he did not take
flight, stampede, or run amok.

"What are you doing here?" Frances broke the spell.

"Raising money," he said, and grinned a feral grin.

At the moment he was raising more than money. She could
see that there was life beneath the towel. Frances drew back, in
prey to some alarm. The lion, who has many noble beauties, is
also equipped with mighty teeth and claws. The lion before her
had a mighty organ, which could do harm if the brute were
teased or frightened. Frances named her anxiety: What if the
towel should fall? Worse than fall—he might unfurl the towel
and drop it, and she did not have a polished shield such as
Perseus carried, or a pocket mirror, or a piece of foil or tin. She
would be forced to confront the Member unreflected, and its
gaze would convert her into solid stone.

"Close your mouth," said the beast. "Unless you're trapping
flies."

"I think you're Paul Treat," said Frances. "Where is
Madeline?"

Paul Treat gave a sheepish smile and brushed his mustache as
if he had finished a meal and was cleaning off the crumbs.

"All gone," he said, and patted his fur-clad stomach.

Frances tried to look stern. He required a sharp rebuke. She glared and frowned, but her body shook with laughter. Little Madeline would make him such a tender morsel. Dressed for the oven, she would look like a quail or a pullet, to be served up on fried toast rounds with sprigs of parsley.

"Where is she?" repeated Frances. "Is she out?"

"At the bank," said Paul. "She's dipping into capital."

"No!" gasped Frances. "You ought to be ashamed."

Paul looked down his nose. "I didn't ask. She offered."

Frances was very hungry, but more offended. She was only three inches taller than swindled Madeline, but she faced the naked giant with resolution. If he had been wearing lapels, she would have grabbed and shaken them.

"You promised her something. You must have. You turned her head."

"It was easy," said Paul. "I waved my magic wand."

Frances blushed. She pretended she did not understand. It would take the luster off her moral indignation if she bandied coarse phrases and traded in double meanings. It was unwise to encourage allusions to his scepter, so precariously covered with a damp white towel.

"I'm paying," said Paul. "I'm paying through the nose. She gets a cut of the gross and a hefty chunk of me."

Frances huffed and puffed. "There must be other ways."

Paul gave her a human look. She did not like it. He might be thinking that she was on his side. Perhaps she was. Poor Faust, stripped of his honor, pledging his pelt to guarantee his art. That midget Mephistopheles known as Madeline had never been bested in her business dealings. Her lawyers would draw up pacts that mortgaged him forever, to be signed in blood and marrow as well as ink.

"Don't take it," said Frances. Her voice sounded too urgent.

Paul was pressing two fingers on the pulse of his left wrist. "You're a towhead," he said. "Your hair is very pretty."

At once Frances raised her hand to smooth her bangs, as if he had said "Your hair is very messy." She remembered she had not thought to use mascara. Without it, her eyes appeared completely lashless. Paul had plentiful lashes and curling reddish eyebrows. His lower lip was fuller than the upper. His long teeth showed when he smiled or spoke. He shifted his weight, his hand still on his wrist. He did not move, but he might move without warning.

Frances measured the second-floor landing with her eyes. Was it four and half feet wide, or only four? She cast a wild glance from one end to the other, as if the way up and down were barricaded. She did not want to have strong feelings in close quarters. Defending Madeline, she had been immune. Was she flagging in her role as Madeline's champion? Little Daniel, like Frances, must have lost his faith, if only for a fraction of a second, when he heard the boulders rolling into place, closing him up inside the cavern with the lion.

Visions of eggs and wheat toast tempted Frances, scrambled eggs and toast with wild thyme honey, or the quince preserves that Madeline kept in stock on the top shelf of a cabinet in the pantry. There were worse things than going hungry until lunchtime. It looked like a matter of eating or being eaten. At that moment the front door opened and slammed loudly. There was a sharp report, like a box dropped on the floor. Frances fled upstairs without taking her leave. She did not look back or she would have observed Paul Treat darting like a frightened hare into the bathroom.

Frances lay low for the rest of the afternoon, except for a foray to the corner store. Skipping breakfast had given her an appetite for processed foods, especially products containing emulsifiers and sweeteners, with flavor boosters, fillers, and extenders, and coloring that was never found in nature. She lined her purchases in rows on her kitchen counter and surveyed them with a shiver of delight: marshmallows (miniature), olive loaf, false whipped cream; bars of milk chocolate, cheese-spread, frozen pound cake; ice cream with splinters of mint, and graham crackers (the only wholesome article in her hoard). She felt as wicked as if she had got them by shoplifting, when in fact she had paid a highway robber's price. She rolled slices of olive loaf and ate them with her fingers, wondering if she should have bought pickle-and-pimento as well. After olive loaf for hors d'oeuvres, what about the main course? Cheese-spread on pound cake? Whipped topping on ice cream? Or all of them mushed together in a soup? Out of her memory came a recipe for s'mores: two grahams, with chocolate and marshmallows in between. The filling should be melted over a campfire, and the sandwich eaten while it is too hot. Frances built four s'mores and wrapped them in tinfoil. She switched on the broiler and watched the coils turn red.

Glorious s'mores. They singed the tongue and fingers. They ran down the chin and formed a brown goatee. Greedy persons like Frances inserted more marshmallows, which began to melt on contact with the heat. She finished one s'more and reached out for another. With the sandwich halfway to her mouth, she saw Paul Treat. He was peering over the banister toward her kitchen. He wavered between advancing and withdrawing, then took one more step and reached the highest stair. The tables were turned. He had captured the advantage. She had caught him in a towel; now he caught her in clown face, with a chocolate muzzle and marshmallow stripes on her cheeks. Should she hold up a veil of tinfoil to hide her face? Or offer him a s'more and watch his face get smudgy? Before she was able to make the right decision, he had entered the kitchen and seized her by the shoulders. He held her firmly and kissed her on the mouth, taking his time, like a chocolate-loving vampire. When he finished, his mouth and whiskers were perfectly clean. Frances felt as if parts of her face had been kissed away. From somewhere downstairs Madeline started calling. She did not have to call more than once before Paul disappeared.

Frances was shocked and surprised to be alive, like a bird in the grip of a cat who drops his prey, having heard his mistress setting out his dinner or having eaten too many birds in the course of the day. She checked herself for specific erotic feelings. Was Eros making her stomach ache, or going hungry? She thought she should try to recall the kiss in detail, but found her memory balked at the assignment. In fact, she had a form of mild amnesia, like the victim of a nasty fall or motor accident.

Frances inspected the three uneaten cookies. They were past their prime. The filling had congealed. She wiped her mouth, which was still on her face, with the corner of a dishtowel. She felt glum and a little cheated, but whether of Paul or her feast she could not make out. She wondered if he had come upstairs to see her, or if he was only exploring Madeline's house. She was not sure she liked the idea of his roaming free. Would it be wiser to spend the night at the nearest hotel? She would have admitted, if she had chosen to question her feelings, that she liked even less the idea that his visit was casual.

In the days that followed the chocolate-marshmallow kiss, Paul Treat began to trouble Frances's sleep, causing dreams of falling, flying, capsizing, and drowning; one nightmare in which she was bandaging his feet; and another, in the small hours of the morning, in which Madeline was flattened outside the window like a moth. In the clearest dream of all, if it was a dream, she woke up, or believed she was awake, to see the door of her bedroom closing, but not latched. She remembered, or dreamed she remembered, closing her door, and thinking of propping a chair underneath the doorknob. When she got up that morning, she forgot her dream or vision, until she noticed that the bedroom door was still ajar. She ascribed her restless night to a new neurosis: Fear of the Taboo Paul.

Taboo, but underfoot, to her discomfort. Madeline's house had become a rehearsal hall. Actors and actresses sat in a queue on the staircase, waiting to read for parts in *A Midsummer Night's Dream*. By day Paul held auditions in the living room; by night he conferred with designers and engineers. From the hall Frances caught a glimpse of Paul presiding. He sat on a high-backed chair, a king at court. Madeline sat by his side, cross-legged on a hassock, swaying with importance like the caterpillar in *Alice*. Paul clasped his right wrist with his left hand and jiggled one knee. He held on to his wrist while he gestured or scratched his beard. Frances had also seen him at the telephone, dialing with his wrist clasped. She thought perhaps he had a nervous tic. Paul clung to his wrist like a lifeline. Every pair of eyes in the room was riveted to his wrist. When he tried to unbutton his jacket with one hand, Frances heard an intake of breath in every throat. The actor who was reading for Puck stopped in midsentence. Paul tried to yank one sleeve down without letting go. Then he snatched his hand away from his wrist and tore off his jacket. Twelve people, along with bystanders in the hallway, exhaled in chorus.

The house was full of motley people and strange behaviors. Frances felt like a visitor from a backward nation, hailing as she did from Cincinnati and the Harwood Press. In her parent cultures, men did not set their hair in curlers, and women never

wore tights and leotards on the street. At home or at Harwood,
men did not greet women with a tweak of the nipple, and no
one kept the door to the bathroom open in order to pursue a
conversation with the other sex. Frances was used to writers and
their ilk; she had never seen theatre people at close hand. Writers were shy and mannerly, unless in liquor. They looked and
acted like poor relations, hoping for acceptance. Writers wore
old clothes, since they did not go to work, but you could see that
their shabby garments had once passed muster. Theatre people
did not hover at the edges of polite society; they camped on the
untracked wilds outside its gates.

Camping is what they were doing in Madeline's kitchen, in
Madeline's hallway, and eventually in rooms upstairs. They
took naps on the carpet and ate sandwiches carried in knap-
sacks. They changed clothes in the open and didn't take cover
for kissing, although some of the kissing would have melted the
wax on the floors. They prowled around muttering audibly or
under their breath, trying to learn long passages by heart. One
young man was delivering his lines to the full-length mirror. A
redheaded girl had concocted a tunic with the kitchen curtains.
Like patients in mental wards or toddlers in play groups, they
did not seem to know they were in a public setting.

After a few days of passing among them without incident,
Frances no longer feared that her nipple might be pinched.
They smiled at her and seemed to take her for granted; and one
older woman, a candidate for Hippolyta, asked Frances if she
could spare some time to cue her. Frances began to bring home
bags of apples, which she piled in a bowl on the table in the hall.
Actors waited long hours and neglected their nutrition, and
some of them went without food to pay for coaching. When one
of them got a paycheck, it was cause for a party. The paid person
treated the others, including Frances, who often had supper on
the rug or on the staircase, eating cold cuts and three-bean salad

with her fingers. None of the cast knew her name, and no one asked it. They offered her food without needing to classify or place her. She thought the world of the theatre might be an ideal democracy, unlike Harwood, where rank was played down but understood. The world outside, with its governments and newspapers, bore no reference to this community of players, just as memories of the home port grow dim for passengers on a cruise ship. When the cruise is over, and the play has had its run, its members make vows to meet but never do so. This analogy gratified Frances, for whom most friendships were tethers to selves she wished she had discarded. Here she was friendly with everyone but close to no one. She was as new to herself as she was to her newfound friends.

More and more, Frances stayed downstairs until quite late. She played poker with Mustardseed, Peaseblossom, Cobweb, and Moth. Hippolyta and Hermia taught her to use eye shadow. Bottom, who was Japanese, told her fortune with rice. When the actors were dismissed, Frances crept into the privy council, where Paul passed judgment on costume designs and sets. One night she watched Puck, who had been asked to stay after rehearsal, standing on a ground cloth wearing brief yellow underpants. Paul, who was dressed in a pin-striped banker's suit, pushed back his cuffs and picked up a house painter's brush. He painted a yellow band around Puck's middle, brushing yellow on the tops of his thighs and on his forearms. Then he found a clean brush and a new can of body paint, and striped Puck's chest and his upper arms in orange. The costume designer twisted his hair in a bun, seized a fresh brush, and slapped green on Puck's legs and feet. The makeup girl smeared red on Puck's face, neck, and shoulders. By the end of the painting session Puck was a rainbow. Paul wanted to shave his head; Puck preferred a red wig.

The next night, Lysander and Demetrius modeled flashing

codpieces. Paul himself sewed the little light bulbs on the pouches. The bulbs were attached by wires to dry-cell batteries, mounted with tape on the actors' upper thighs. Lysander, whose thighs were sweaty, made nervous jokes about electrocution. Paul showed him the switch on the battery, and told him to recite part of a love scene, pushing the switch when a verse expressed secret lechery. At first he flashed without regard to meaning ("Hear me, Hermia, I have a widow aunt"); then he lit up like fireflies in July, allowing the urgent words no tender shadings. "Less is more!" shouted Paul, and ran him through his paces until he could flash and speak with some proportion. Then Paul read the woman's part without a script and taught Demetrius how to work his codpiece. It grew late and Frances had to go to bed, so she never heard the outcome of a quarrel over whether the wires and batteries should show, or whether they should be discreetly hidden.

Frances was keeping unaccustomed hours. She walked through the day in a blue haze of fatigue. The fall catalogue was due and she owed it thirteen entries. She broke lunch dates and tried to nap on her office sofa, which had wooden arms and a pillow that had lost its stuffing. Every evening she swore she would march herself upstairs, and each time she broke her vow and stayed below. If she had yielded to a mortal appetite for sleep, she might have missed Puck in his skin of many colors.

The night after the flashing britches, Paul was absent. She thought his bag of tricks must be depleted. Before she collected her purse and her file of papers, she glanced into the living room with blurred, myopic eyes. The director's chair was occupied. She blinked. If Paul had come in, she would have seen or sensed him. She took a step forward. The occupant was not Paul, unless he had fallen into a vat of lime or acid. Sitting erect, with both feet on the floor, was a skeleton wearing a microphone like a pendant. She looked more closely. No dirt clung to the bones, which were brownish, not white, the color of darkened varnish. Frances was relieved. Theatre folk could be ruthless in the name of production values; she did not think their zeal would extend to robbing graves. These old bones must have starred in many anatomy lessons, copied and handled by budding docs or artists. The skeleton was being groomed for another lead. The costume designer covered him with black velvet, draping his skull so his noseless face was hooded. The technical director fixed the wires from the microphone to a standing mike plugged in across the room. Oberon, a stocky actor with chapped red cheeks, tested the system, reciting random lines: "Ill met by moonlight, proud Titania." . . . "Hie therefore, Robin, overcast the night." The skeleton echoed his ventriloquist in hollow tones.

The glass door opened, banging the picture window. Paul stepped in from the garden with Madeline behind him. "It sucks!" he roared. "Cute as catshit! I want Oberon live." Only Oberon, the actor, was pleased. The rest of the crew protested the change profanely. Oberon, the skeleton, chose that moment to fall off his chair, clattering to the ground, breaking one spiny foot as he tumbled. "Jesus Christ in a bucket," swore Paul. "There goes eight hundred big ones." "It's an omen," said Leo, the propman. "We broke him, we own him." "I'm the director," said Paul. "I say we go live."

Frances wanted to express an opinion. She caught herself raising her hand, like a child in the classroom. Why did the skeleton suck? The boys had bulbs in their crotches. Why did Paul keep yelling "Gimmick!", if Puck's skin was painted? Frances was naïve when it came to such fine distinctions, but she learned as she listened to Paul scorning his invention. It seemed that wiring the bones for sound did not serve the play; it just made the director look like a clever fellow. It was like doing

Hamlet in blackface or *Lear* in zoot suits, and referring to your bright idea as a "production concept." She recalled what she had read or heard of Paul's previous works. The same critics who called him a genius said he went too far. Frances disagreed. It was clear to her now that Paul did not make mistakes: Peer Gynt ought to walk on stilts; the lovers in *As You Like It* needed seals for mascots. Frances was on the brink of a conversion. How benign Paul was, how wise, how democratic, letting his crew voice their uninspired opinions. Genius has no need to offer an accounting, but a good leader never stifles his subjects' fervor. Did the crew give Paul due credit for his genius? Were they aware, from their short-sighted perspective, that he had pledged his life to the highest form of art? A tragic form, like sculpting in ice, since nothing was left of the most renowned productions but newspaper clippings, memories, and still photographs. Now that Paul had opened her eyes, Frances found little pleasure in books. For one thing, books came in such limited color schemes: white for the pages; black print; one stain for the binding. Books had no musical background and no lighting effects. To read that Peter Pan could fly was dull next to seeing him move by invisible wires across a stage. A writer could not do a forest with one potted tree. Writers described the bark, the leaves, the earth, the time of day, using up paragraphs that the reader skimmed or skipped. Writers drove their imaginations like work-worn mules. Modern writers took the quick way out, in fantasy, making up girls furred and clawed like beasts, men who walked on their heads, hermaphrodites of mixed religions, and other characters burdened with meaning, and hence faceless. No wonder writers needed endless praise and constant pep talks. They were playing for the pot of gold with a pair of deuces. Holding a loser's hand makes the player nervous. Did Frances want to keep the job of backing losers? It was as

insolent to say she would rather be backing Paul as to say sh
would rather back Etna or Mauna Loa. One light bulb basted
at the groin was worth a thousand words.

Frances put herself on automatic pilot in the daytime. She used
the part of her brain reserved for menial chores. She worked
faster because the work seemed unimportant, and was re-
warded with extra tasks by her boss, Ham Griner. When she
finished these tasks, she locked horns with Panda Wattel, who
wanted an orchidlike vulva, or a vulvalike orchid, on her jacket.
Panda changed her mind with the speed of a torpedo when
Frances asked her to imagine saying "vulva" to Mr. Harwood.

Frances lived for the nights and each night she drew closer,
leaving her station by the living-room door and approaching the
action, growing bold enough to take up space on the only sofa, in
a seat that was usually saved for the assistant director. Seated
where she was, she was drawn into the action. She was a pair of
hands when the company was shorthanded. She hemmed the
lovers' wedding capes, though she was no seamstress, and glued
false lashes on Bottom's ass's head. Once Paul dumped the
promptbook in her lap and asked her to run the lines at a rapid
tempo. Madeline, who sat by Paul in a zippered lounging costume, decided that Frances was being unduly favored. She took
over the promptbook and sent her to make coffee.

One night, Frances sat winding yarn for the lion's mane. Paul
was working with Lysander, who was apt to freeze during love
scenes. Hermia had left; she only made things worse. Either
Hermia—or Paul, who kept hounding him: "Two bosoms,
man, two bosoms and one troth! That's her tits—forget Shakespeare, think tits! Take a feel, go on, she's got nice ones, you
don't mind, do you, doll?" Hermia, yawning from boredom,

had clapped his hand to her breast and held it firmly. A brief struggle ensued until Lysander broke out of her grasp. "Are you a virgin," said Paul, "or a faggot? Clear the room! He can't do it for a crowd." Frances picked up her yarn and started to leave with the others. "You stay here," said Paul. "We can use you." He turned to Lysander. "Look at her. She's built like a kid. No knockers to scare you." Lysander smiled bravely at Frances, as if to make up for Paul's churlish appraisal of her measurements. Frances smiled back. This was professional theatre. Professionals had to grow hardened to personal remarks.

Madeline walked in with a glass and a bottle and sat in Paul's chair. An injunction to empty the room did not include investors. Paul was pacing, clasping his wrist, and pressing three fingers of his free hand on the vein in his temple. Frances observed him. Plugging into two major pulses must make his mind sharper. "O.K., sit," ordered Paul. "Hold it. Frances. Douse those lights. Wait. I'll do it." With one corner lamp burning, the lighting was dim, but kinder. Frances and Lysander waited mutely for further instructions. "On the rug," Paul said. "Green rug equals grassy turf." Paul sat down with his back against the wall, about twelve feet away. It was the distance, if the room were a theatre, from the front row to the lip of the stage. "You're an actor," said Paul to Lysander. "Anything you do in private, you can do in public." Lysander nodded, or twitched. His eyes were shut, like a patient getting an injection. Frances felt sorry for her timid partner. He had a sweet face, with an undeveloped nose. For a small nose, it harbored a lot of reddish spots.

Nothing had been heard from Paul for several minutes. There was no sound except wine glugging into Madeline's glass. Frances began to wish he would bark directions, but Lysander took some courage from his silence. All at once, Lysander made some sneaky moves: a hand on her thigh; a buttock eased against her; breath on her cheek; a definite change in breathing. Frances had heard that the kind of exercise they were doing was called an improvisation, or an "improv," in which the actors are given a theme, but no plan or script. Improvs gave proof of an actor's imagination; anything might happen if both partners could free their instruments. It was clear that Lysander was involved in freeing his. He was kissing Frances on the ear and inching toward her mouth. He was kissing her on the lips and tilting her backward. He was working on her buttons and trying to unhook her waistband. Frances wished, in the clinch, that she had taken instrument lessons. He had captured the lead and she might never get it back. If she had the initiative, how could she swing things her way? What was her way? She had none, only pleasing Paul. Paul ought to be pleased. Lysander had lost his shyness. Lysander had his hand on the tab of his own zipper. The sound of the zipper unzipping could be heard in China.

"Paul?" It was Madeline talking. "Paul! Make them stop!"

"What?" answered Paul. His voice was rough and distant as if he had been roused from a catnap or a trance.

"Not in my house," said Madeline. "You make them stop!"

"Good," said Paul. "Very real. You both did good."

Lysander spit on his hands and smoothed down his hair. He zipped himself up and went over to get his knapsack. He walked with an upright spine and a springy step. As he left, he clapped Frances on the shoulder, by way of thanks. Thanks to Lysander, Frances's skirt was on backward. Her shirttails were showing and her tights sagged in folds at the knees. She never regained full control of her twisted clothing. She did not say good night to Paul when she left the room.

Frances prepared herself to run the gauntlet, but nobody was sitting in the hall or on the stairs. She felt, nonetheless, that a thousand eyes were upon her, so she looked straight ahead and walked with her chin up high, like the Scarlet Woman being led to the stocks in Salem. The closer she got to her rooms, the more she slumped. When she reached the top floor, her chin had dropped to her chest. She sat on the bed, in her creased, disobedient garments. She made no attempt to undress and change into her nightclothes, since her physical discomfort matched the confusion in her mind. A professional actress would not have conflicting reactions; she would straighten her clothes, go home, and gargle with mouthwash. She might ask herself what she had learned from the improvised love scene; she would not keep replaying the scene with corrected endings involving the discovery of an ice pick or a dagger on her person. She would never expect the director to cut the scene short, or to respect the maidenly modesty of one of his cast.

On the whole, Frances thought she was safer in the world of letters. Writers thought things up by themselves. Writers' minds might resemble a spook house full of cobwebs and severed limbs, but writers never invited live people to come into their studies and act out bloody scenes. Writers might ill-treat themselves and their nervous systems; they did not push volunteers or hirelings past the breaking point. Frances knew some tall male writers. She knew some handsome ones. Some of these manly writers wished to know her, too. The better she knew them, the more she observed a likeness. They were her brother worms. They were hypocrites and hiders. They bit their nails and ground their teeth while sleeping. They never got revenge, except in stories. They took no risks, except on ruled white paper. Paul was of another species altogether. If he kept a list of enemies in his wallet, he would not read it over and over again, in secret, until the paper was split from folding and refolding. He would punish his enemy, cross his name off the list, add new names, and strike them out in turn. Eventually he would need a fresh sheet of paper. Her name had no chance of appearing on his enemies list. If it did, it would mean she had managed to attract his notice. Why would a ruddy lion take stock of a worm? Frances wished she could be content with her own kind, but a worm may look at a lion, like a cat at a king. She might look at the king of beasts, but she might not yearn. In a contest for grotesque mismatings, the prize would go to worm and lion.

Frances wanted a bath. She pulled off her clothes and stuffed them into a trash bag. She leaned over the tub and adjusted the hot and cold faucets. She stepped in, armed with brushes and cloths, like a housewife embarked on spring-cleaning. She turned red from the heat of the water and the effort of scrubbing. She brushed the soles of her feet, her knees and elbows. She scoured her bosoms and buttocks, using three different lathers. When she emerged from the bath, she had shed several layers of skin.

Frances had left her bathrobe in the bedroom. She noticed that a light was burning in her kitchen. As she started toward the kitchen, she heard stairs creak behind her. The tread was heavy. The footfall was not Madeline's. She wheeled around.

"I want to see your fruits," said Paul.

As if to oblige him, Frances lost control of her towel. One of her fruits was uncovered, and before her numb fingers could gather the corners of the cloth, the other was exposed.

"Pink nipples," said Paul. "Not brown." He was clutching his wrist. He held it so tightly that the veins in his hands stood out.

"What are you doing?" asked Frances, pointing at his wrist.

"Taking my pulse," he said.

"You do it all the time."

"I might be dead," said Paul. "I have to check."

Frances approached him. His complexion was pale by nature. If he was able to speak, it argued he must be breathing. Perhaps he had a phobia. She had heard of a painter who was frightened by a shade of blue, and a poet who believed his pen was made of glass. She wondered if her fruits had induced a phobic reaction. She had less to fear if Paul was afraid of her.

"Madeline," said Frances, naming one object of dread.

"Asleep," said Paul. "Tanked up." He looked disapproving.

"She's a very poor sleeper," said Frances, peering over the railing.

"Can I feel them?" asked Paul. He backed up, instead of advancing.

Frances was surprised. This was the very person who had shamed Lysander, and taunted him for having girlish scruples. She lowered the towel and tucked it around her waist.

"All right," said Frances. "You're going to need both hands." She offered up her breasts on her palms, like pears on plates.

Paul resembled bashful Lysander as Hamlet was mad—north-northwest. At every other point of the compass he needed no coaching. The prevailing winds favored loss of inhibition. Her towel was not tied to survive such a lusty gale. Paul handled and tasted her, choosing the sweetest sections, like a restaurant chef sampling produce at a market garden. "Choice," he said, between mouthfuls, praising her mound. "Small but delicious," he said as he savored her globes. Frances wondered why Hemingway had written that no man can make love very long in a standing position. Did the blood leave their heads as it rushed to their pleasure centers? Paul showed no signs of dizziness or faulty balance, although sometimes he kneeled, which might keep him from feeling light-headed. Nothing was required of Frances except standing still. Her guest was doing the work. Was she a proper hostess? Wasn't she remiss, detaining her guest in the hallway? Wouldn't it be friendlier to lead the way to the bedroom? Etiquette books drew a veil over cases like this one, though tradition decreed, in the matter of sexual exchanges, that it was up to the man to take the first step toward the bed. It was typical of Hemingway to ascribe greater urgency to men. It was Frances who was giddy, and Paul who had perfect equilibrium. She was ready for closure, but he seemed content with preamble. She wondered if Paul kept Madeline on short rations. Did Madeline need to drink wine in order to sleep? Madeline was altered lately, subdued and moodier. Perhaps Frances's temperature went down, when she thought of Madeline, or perhaps Paul had thought of her, too, since he straightened his tie and brushed off the knees of his trousers. Frances watched him preparing for departure. She had no clothing to adjust. Her damp towel was lying on the floor. Paul picked up the towel, folded it in thirds, and gave it back to her.

"I'm not finished," he said, molding her haunches and squeezing them. "Perhaps you're the girl of my dreams. You're not like other women."

"I am too!" she retorted, as if Paul had meant to insult her.

"No, you're not," answered Paul. "I see through you. You're only pretending."

Frances opened her mouth to protest her mediocrity more loudly. Paul was already making an exit, attempting to cross the hall silently. When he reached the top stair, he dropped out of sight very fast. While he made his way down, she did not hear the staircase creak once.

The next day was Saturday, the day Frances kept for Edie. Edie liked to turn every activity into a tradition, so she knew what she was doing for weeks, even months, in advance: Saturday for Frances, Sunday dinner with Hill and his parents, Monday at the fertility clinic, Tuesday evening for subscription tickets,

Thursday for errands. Her calendar never varied except for Wednesdays, though she had tried many times to beat Wednesdays into shape. Frances disliked making plans, so she fit into Edie's. Sometimes she looked down the years and saw a chain of Saturdays, unbroken unless she left town or changed her identity. Saturdays began at noon, in Edie's apartment. They ate tuna-fish salad; then Frances watched Edie do chores: bits of ironing or mending; flushing clogged fountain pens with water; chopping up vegetables for supper; mothproofing winter clothes. Today Edie was polishing spoons with salt and vinegar. Frances sat on a kitchen chair and drank black coffee. She had sat up most of the night on a softer chair, reading the later poems of Wallace Stevens, in an effort to purify and elevate her fevered mind. Edie was never distracted by domestic tasks. When her hands were busy, she was freer to close in on Frances. Frances felt it coming, but she saw it from a distance; her fatigue was a buffer, like sandbags piled around a fort.

"Hill's brother knows Paul Treat," said Edie, rinsing out a sponge. She had finished the silver spoons and started on the knives. "I mean, he knows a girl he dumped. He owes her money."

"Hill's brother?"

Edie sniffed. "She says he owns a shotgun."

"Who's 'he'?" said Frances. "What's the antecedent?"

"You ought to know. You said you let him kiss you."

Frances made a show of blowing on her coffee. Each confession she had made to Edie came back to haunt her, though it was more important to know what not to tell her. Frances paid out information like a tithe, little disclosures as a cover for the big ones. Over the years, the minor confessions had mounted up until Edie could be said to have the goods on Frances. Edie recorded information and played it back distorted, with her bias or approbation factored in. Edie kept a file on Frances, under rigid headings. The person in the file was like, yet not like, Frances. The dossier described her fears, her quirks, her failures; it did not include her triumphs over weakness. Was kissing Paul a triumph or a failure? Did Frances need Edie to tell her which was which? Was Frances, who was unmarried, a speeding car, and Edie the voice of reason, or braking system?

Edie had been watching Frances during this rumination.

"Is that all he did, is kiss you?"

"Yes," said Frances. She didn't even have to cross her fingers, since Edie had not asked where or how, but only whether.

"Does Madeline know?" asked Edie, pouring more vinegar.

"That's the last thing I'd do."

"You wouldn't. But maybe he did." Edie added salt to the mixture and stirred it up. "You'll lose your apartment. You'll be put out on the street."

Frances had visions of forty-five–point tabloid headlines, picked up by the wires and featured in Cincinnati. She foresaw her ultimate ruin and disgrace: fired from Harwood, shunned by decent people. Edie continued stirring while Frances writhed. She dipped a knife and wiped it. She dipped another.

"Would you like Paul Treat if he didn't belong to Madeline?"

Frances gripped the seat of her chair as if it were sliding. From the back, Edie seemed to have swelled, like a witch or a toad.

"You took Preston away from Hatsy. In case you've forgotten."

Frances gathered her wits. Did she know someone called Hatsy? Short for Harriet? Harriet. Braids. Crossed eyes. Scabbed kneecaps. Harriet Day, whose nurse walked her to school. No one else had a nurse by the time they were in fourth grade. Preston was harder to fish from the ooze of memory. Out he came, floating belly upward, with his shirttails torn and his socks around his ankles. She remembered his little rat teeth and his crimpy hair, and his habit of sneaking up and trying to hug her, while he only punched chubby Hatsy in the stomach. Frances began to laugh as she swallowed coffee. The coffee shot up her nose and made her sneeze. Branded for life! Strayed from the path in childhood! The sins of the playground had dogged her all these years.

Edie stopped cleaning knives and watched her snorting. "You think you can get away with murder, Frances."

In spite of her coloring, Frances never blushed, but she felt a wave of heat from top to toe, as if the blush were taking place within her. Edie's flat stare held all of public opinion, or at least the opinion of the people Frances came from. Was consorting with directors a crime to these good people? Bankers and brokers kissed girls, and so did lawyers. Some of that kissing led to copulation, which often occurred outside the bonds of wedlock. If kissing directors was tantamount to murder, then mating with them was equated with high treason. Mating with directors (or merchants, masseurs, or poets, or clergy of fundamentalist persuasions) was a tribal crime, not punishable by law, but only by ostracism and dismissal.

Edie had turned her back to wash the knives. She dried them on a linen towel, freshly washed and ironed. Now she was blamelessly tasting a pot of soup, a meatless dish that she made with roots and greens. Frances decided to make a false confession, or, rather, to gratify Edie's darkest inklings. It would not be the same as telling a flagrant lie, since she, if not Paul, had been guilty in intention. She preferred to be hanged for outright fornication. Kissing was too small an offense to merit banishment. Besides, she enjoyed a chance for deviling Edie. Hill Childs wore pajamas to bed, as well as earplugs.

"You were right," said Frances. "We did it. We made the beast."

The soup scalded Edie's tongue. She dropped her spoon.

"Backwards. And sideways. And sitting in a chair." Edie was coughing. "Should I hit you on the back?

"My, yes," said Frances. "We did forbidden things." She stretched and yawned. "Do you know what men like best?" Edie raised her spoon. "Of course. You must. You're married. I'm a rookie at sex. It's all old hat to you."

Edie left the stove and edged a little closer. Frances had hoisted her legs up on the table. Edie pushed Frances's feet off the tabletop. She rubbed the surface with a towel and checked it for scratches.

"What kind of chair?" said Edie, who went on rubbing.

"Armless," said Frances, patting the chair she was sitting on. "A boudoir chair would be nicer. Lower to the ground."

"Who sits where?" asked Edie.

"Man on chair. Girl on man," said Frances.

"Facing the man?" said Edie. "Or turned away?"

"That's a thought," said Frances. "You could try it facing out. Why not?"

Edie's neck was red. Her eyebrows met in the middle. She had never asked Frances for pointers of an intimate nature. She had never asked Frances for advice on any subject. Sex, as a topic, was a leveler and an equalizer. Here was Edie, getting down to worm level with Frances. From now on they might communicate as one worm to another.

Not for long. Edie tucked in her blouse and stood up smartly, routing Frances's hopeful visions of worms together.

"People talk," said Edie. "You need a paying job. You don't have a private income like your landlady."

Frances was ambushed. She searched for some rejoinder. "I might be in love," she said. "Is that better or worse?"

"When she kicks you out," Edie said, "you can have our guest room."

"I wish you were on my side. Just once," said Frances.

"I do my best," said Edie. "You always fight me."

Frances walked home, or, rather, back to Madeline's. She took the long way around, going through the park. The day was clear and breezy, but her sails were drooping. Taking the wind out of her sails was Edie's role. Sometimes Frances got bright ideas and wayward notions. Whenever she did, Edie steered her back in line. Edie saw danger lurking in Frances's daydreams. A friend had the duty of fostering the good in her friend. Frances wished she could find a friend who would sponsor the worst. Normal friends clapped their hands in glee when a man had kissed you. They asked if he was good at kissing. They asked if he had promised to call again, and when. They offered to lend you their new dress, or their best pearl earrings. Since they loved you, they took it for granted that men would love you. If the man defaulted, they blamed his vision, not your attractions. Where the man saw a worm, they would see a fairy princess. In time, under the kind protection of such friends, you might straighten your spine and pick up your crown and scepter. On the other hand, friends like these might show no judgment. Blinded by love, they might let you aim too high. A worm in a ball gown cuts a foolish figure. Edie would never fasten the hooks and eyes on her ball dress, or powder her shoulders, or pin up stray wisps of hair, but Edie would prevent her from tripping on the sill of the ballroom wearing a pair of glass slippers that were somebody else's size.

Frances paused on Madeline's doorstep and fished out her keys. She opened the door. The house was untidy and empty. The actors had gone, leaving only their caps and sweatshirts. Paul's *Dream* was rehearsing on a proper proscenium stage.

Paul and Madeline got back very late, often well after midnight. Sometimes Madeline came home first, while Paul gave his notes to the cast. When Paul let himself in, Madeline was already sleeping. That meant Paul was at large in the house, and free to wander. Frances wasted no time. She opened the yellow directory in the kitchen and found the number of a locksmith who answered calls on weekends. She used Madeline's phone, since the call was in Madeline's interest. She ordered one dead-bolt lock and a sliding chain lock for her bedroom, and a doorknob containing a button lock for the bathroom. The locksmith in question charged higher fees for emergencies. Frances did not argue. Her case qualified as urgent.

All that week Frances tried to work but came out losing. Boxes of manuscripts piled up on her bottom shelf. When they numbered fourteen, she stacked them on top of her desk. In order to clear the space, she would have to read them. Panda Wattel came in for her regular Wednesday meeting. Frances let her win several battles without a fight. Panda's hero would burst into print with a face "famished with anger." In spite of Frances, his eyes would be "green as locusts whizzing."

Frances was late to work, though she stayed after hours. Locks on her bedroom door did not guarantee sleep. She fled from the house in the mornings to avoid Paul Treat, but Wednesday he had loomed up suddenly in the hallway, and cupped one buttock before she could find her keys. Her nerves were shot from dodging Paul and sleeping badly, and hours spent doing expiatory chores. In the evening, when Paul and Madeline were at the theatre, she did the jobs the maid never got around to: sweeping out ashes, scouring the bricks on the hearth, lining the cupboards with paper, polishing shoes.

On Friday morning Frances was even later. Ruthanne gave her a worried look as she hurried in. Ruthanne, who was twenty, thought Frances was middle-aged. Frances had told her her age and Ruthanne had exclaimed, "I hope I look as young as you do when I'm twenty-seven!" Ruthanne protected Frances from whiny phone calls, and stood guard when the office nuisance made his rounds. This morning she had covered Frances's tardy entrance by telling Ham Griner she was meeting with an agent.

Ruthanne brought two cups of coffee on a tray. "Are you feeling all right?" she asked, in a sickroom whisper.

"Well enough," Frances said, "for a person of my years."

"I brought my pad. We ought to do dictation."

"Do we have to?" said Frances. "Watch out. The cups are hot."

Ruthanne dropped her pad without the least reluctance. She had more on her mind than shorthand and dictation. She had spent twenty-five dollars on a worthless psychic reading. The psychic's name was Lockheed, like the airplane. The psychic read palms and worked out of a restaurant. Frances normally took pleasure in Ruthanne's eager chatter. Today she listened, but she could not always claim to hear her. She could hear the odd word, enough to be responsive. At the moment the word she heard was odd indeed.

"Slow down. He said there were pterodactyls in New Jersey?"

"Big Foot in New Jersey," said Ruthanne. "Pterodactyls outside of Houston."

"What's the connection?" said Frances. "Are you going to marry one?"

"He was full of it," said Ruthanne. "He was sipping gin. He told me to hug a tree to cure a headache. He said I had broken windows in my apartment."

"That's a hit," said Frances. "You have two. I remember you told me."

"Oh, great, for twenty-five dollars? Plus I'm going to meet an obese person on the subway. And a negative aura around the letter P."

"Who's P in your life?" asked Frances, leaning forward.

"Not in my life," said Ruthanne. "In my vicinity."

"What sex is P?" said Frances. "Did he mention that?"

"The king of spades," said Ruthanne. "He used cards, too. You know what else? It lasted fifteen minutes."

Frances was sympathetic to Ruthanne's pique. The carto-mancers Frances had consulted seemed to see her as a pane of glass. One turbaned diviner had read right through her, and picked up facts that pertained to her male companion, who was waiting at the bar while Frances took her turn. Another one had spent the session on her mother, forecasting her coming engage-ment and remarriage. Frances might be nine-tenths under water, like an iceberg, but psychics were supposed to sound the hidden depths. No one, either sensitive or obtuse, could mistake Ruthanne for a plain, transparent filter, but what if the P in her reading stood for Paul? And not only Edie but the spirits were set against him? Frances had often relished thwarting Edie; she had no training for doing combat with the Fates.

Maybe the wisest course of action was retreat. She would move out of Madeline's, leaving a false address. She pictured a small apartment, with a metal fire door and windows barred by heavy folding gates, in a building where all the tenants would be strangers, who passed her in the halls and did not smile or greet her. In her new home she could wear few clothes, or none at all. At Madeline's, where she had four separate rooms, she did not usually cross the landing unless she was fully covered. Some-times she peered out the bedroom door to check for traffic, then darted to the bathroom, naked, with her heart in her throat. In her new home she could shed her clothes out in the open, instead of dressing or disrobing behind the closet door. She could loll in the tub and read till the pages wilted, rather than racing through her shower as if she were being clocked. It might be better if her new apartment had no windows, and better still if the apartment had no doors. Paul Treat, that king-size courier of scandal, would never gain entry to her oubliette.

Ruthanne, who had slipped away to get more coffee, came back to call Frances to the weekly meeting. The editorial meeting was held in the conference room, which resembled the dungeon of Frances's cloistral reveries, an airless interior room with dark green walls. The editors sat at a showy rectangular table made of walnut veneer that was finished to reveal the burl, or plastic that looked like varnished burly walnut. Mr. Harwood and Brian Coles had gone to Boston, where the Harwood Press had opened another office, leaving a quorum of four, which meant a nice short session.

Ursula Plumb, who did the "meat and potatoes" books—cookery, needlework, sex, pets, health, and children—always came to these meetings with something to busy her hands. Today she had set a fig plant by her chair, so she could examine its leaves for spider mites and aphids. If Mr. Harwood had been present, she would have brought a smaller plant, her mother-of-thousands or silver-leaf begonia. The editor-in-chief, Hammy Griner, took his seat at the head of the table. Margaret Learned sat on his right and Frances on his left, leaving Ursula quarantined down at the other end. Hammy, who was pink and chubby, was afflicted with allergies. He was apt to swell up from the smallest insect bite. He began to scratch as soon as he crossed the threshold, although Ursula had explained that aphids do not bite people. Neither Margaret nor Frances trusted this explanation.

"You can't kill them all," said Margaret. "They have to go somewhere."

"They land on me," said Hammy, whose eyes were running.

"I see one," said Frances, whomping a speck on her notebook.

"Nonsense," said Ursula briskly. "I never miss." As she spoke, she whisked an atomizer out of her handbag, sprayed the leaf she had just been cleaning, and wiped it with a handkerchief, a well-used handkerchief, crumpled and blotted with lipstick.

Hammy was sneezing and Margaret was growing restless. Margaret ran the meetings, since Hammy had not finished college and she had done all the work for her doctorate except the thesis. Margaret's credentials were probably a powerful allergen, more vexing to Hammy's system than Ursula's aphids.

"I'm sure you're familiar with Arvid Korn," said Margaret. "Arvid is a distinguished Lyman Fellow." Margaret's authors were always eminent or distinguished. They were also top men in their fields and seminal influences.

"Of course. Oh, yes," said Hammy. "A first-rate mind."

"What's the proposal?" asked Frances, tapping her pencil.

"'The Role of the Jews in the Dissident Labor Movement.'"

"Oh, snore," said Frances, sinking down in her chair. Margaret took this rude reaction in good part. She dropped an eraser into Frances's cup of coffee.

"No more dissident Jews," said Ursula, who kept informed. "There are two in the stores, and one in the works at Harper's."

"Arvid Korn," said Hammy, looking a bit more cheerful. "Nephew of Isaiah Berlin on his mother's side. Married Lionel Trilling's sister. Or Irving Howe's. Divorced her for Alfred Kazin's second cousin."

Academic genealogy was Hammy's passion. He knew family trees on the paternal and distaff sides. He knew the names of department chairmen back to Louis Agassiz. Tenured professors were dukes and earls to Hammy. Poor Hammy. He looked at Margaret for approval. He would have died in bliss if she had stooped to gossip with him. She ignored him by pretending to collate Korn's proposal. Hammy was not important to Margaret's career. She did not need his consent to sign an author. She went over his head and appealed to Mr. Harwood, who was more frightened of her erudition than his chief editor.

Frances had never made grown men quail for any reason, so she rather admired this talent in Margaret Learned. She would have admired it more if Margaret had picked on bullies; Mr. Harwood and Hammy were patient, courteous fellows. Margaret never encroached on Frances's own domain, though her reasons were hardly flattering to Frances. Margaret was often heard to make the statement that fiction provided no fodder for the brain, since it was full of unsystematic speculation and facts that would not stand up to careful checking. Occasionally, Frances had caught her reading fiction: *Anna Karenina, Daniel Deronda,* and *Manon Lescaut.* Since each of these novels had proper names for titles, Frances wondered if Margaret thought they were biographies. After clever questioning she had discovered Margaret's formula: Novels were worthwhile if they were over a hundred years old.

Ursula had finished grooming the leaves of the ficus, and turned her attention to grooming her skirt and sweater. Hammy held up his handkerchief like a surgical mask. Ursula plucked off lints and flicked them into space, where the breeze from the baseboard ventilator kept them airborne. Hammy flinched as she flicked, as if he were being bombarded. Ursula brushed at the sides of her skirt to raise more lint. As she slapped the fabric, she also raised some dust. Even a pliant soul like Hammy had his limits. He dropped his handkerchief and hunted in his jacket pockets. After rooting around, he came up with his quarry. He displayed four pasteboard cards with printing on them.

"Oh, no," said Ursula. She had seen their like before. In consternation, she ate a piece of lint.

"Tickets," said Hammy. "For the Dreiser Colony dinner." His voice was stuffy, but his eyes had a vengeful gleam.

The Dreiser Colony was a writers' retreat in Pennsylvania. Every year the board of directors held a benefit, and every year most publishers took a block of tickets. The Harwood table was always filled over loud objections, and Hammy often bartered concessions for attendance, such as excusing Margaret from a sales convention if she promised to drag her husband and two friends.

Hammy dealt out the cards, face up, around the table.

"I can't go," said Frances. "I'm going to have the flu."

Ursula dusted off her ticket as if it, too, had aphids. "Why me?" she said. "I had to go last year. They showed slides of Theodore Dreiser in a rowboat."

"And slides of raccoons eating the writers' box lunches," said Margaret.

"And slides of writers eating the coons' box lunches," said Frances.

"Think about it, friends," said Hammy. "You have a choice. The Dreiser dinner, or Come As Your Muse Night at the Academy."

"Glaaargh," said Frances, miming sudden death.

"I won't take Fred," said Margaret, "and you can't make me."

Hammy started to laugh. In his congested state, it sounded more like choking than amusement. Frances reached over to pat him on the back. In a moment she was laughing, and so was

Margaret. Ursula joined in last, but laughed the loudest. When Ruthanne opened the door, since no one had heard her knock, she found Hammy encircled by three hilarious ladies, one patting his back, another his hand, and the third his pate.

Ruthanne waved at Frances until she caught her eye. Frances gave Hammy an extra pat and came to meet her. Ruthanne looked pale, as if she had bad news. Frances wondered what petty crisis was in the making. Had Panda rejected the sketches for her jacket? Had the copy editor left the Peace Corps memoirs in a taxi?

"What's the trouble, bean?" said Frances. "Tell me slowly."

"It's a P," said Ruthanne. "On the phone. It all came true."

"The king of spades?" asked Frances. "Or the queen?"

"King," said Ruthanne. "He says his name is Paul."

"Why would he lie?" said Frances, acting casual. "I'll take it at my desk. The meeting's over."

Telephone calls were used to make appointments. Paul Treat had never called Frances on the telephone. He had thought of her as a part of Madeline's household; now he saw her as a separate person with a private life. What would she do if he asked for a secret meeting? She might agree to a meeting in a well-lit public place. Frances should have been racing to her office like an eager lover. Instead, she paused at the water fountain to have a drink. She stopped to read the fire-drill regulations and a notice announcing charter flights to Zurich. She was dragging her feet like a prisoner under trial returning to his place in the courtroom to hear the verdict. As she loitered, she was seized with a pang of pure nostalgia, as if her tenure at Harwood were already in the past. She loved the part of her job that resembled village life, orderly, gossipy, civil, and unsurprising. For the sake of their common work and the general good, she and her colleagues found ways to blend and think alike.

They applauded each other's maverick sparks of brilliance. Frances sensed that Paul Treat would disrupt this gracious structure. At rare, odd moments she had heard the voice of the Paul-Within-Her whispering that Frances and Harwood were not a perfect fit. She had thwarted and ignored this crafty inner demon, but an attachment to Paul would give it food and life.

Paul spoke before Frances had barely said hello. "Get over here. Where are Madeline's sleeping pills?"

Frances sat down. Her tongue seemed to be tied. Whatever it was, Paul's mission was not romantic.

"Frances?" Paul's tone was testy. "I've got to find the pills." It was only the second time he had used her name. "They're not in the bathroom. Or on the bedside table. I've had it. I don't need this aggravation."

"Pills," answered Frances, like a gifted parrot.

"I mean it," said Paul. "You get your ass in gear."

"I'm at work," said Frances.

"Thanks a lot," said Paul. "Do you want me to sit around and let her take them?"

The line went dead. Frances stared at the telephone. She forgot to replace the receiver for several moments. For several more, she sat in her chair like a statue. Frances never resisted a plea for aid and service. Why wasn't she tearing out the door and grabbing a taxi? Was Madeline expiring, even as she sat there? Sinking onto piles of pillows edged with lace? This spiteful vision shamed her into action. What kind of weasel had wicked thoughts in an emergency? What kind of person had thoughts at all when help was needed? Frances scribbled a note to Ruthanne, who had gone to lunch. She ran to the lobby, where the elevator doors were opening.

·   ·   ·

Like all row houses, Madeline's house was poorly lit. There were windows at the front and back, but none on the sides. Electric lights were needed in the mornings, as well as in the longest days of summer. Frances arrived at forty-five minutes past noon. When she opened the door, the house was dark and silent. Where was the ambulance? Where were the paramedics? A lifesaving squad created no small commotion. She flew up the stairs and burst into Madeline's room. The room was empty. The bedclothes were smooth and tidy. The bathroom adjoining the bedroom was clean and vacant. Madeline's nightgown was hanging behind the door. Had the rescue team collected the pills and mopped up the vomit? Bagged Madeline in plastic, as naked as the day she was born? Where was Paul, the sorrowing swain, now bereft of his backer? Was he lying in an upper room, following her example? Frances was frightened. If she found him, how could she lift him? How could she carry him and force him to walk off the poison? Frances was not only frightened, but resentful. This is what came of consorting with theatre people. They lived their lives under spotlights. Nothing was private. Suicide attempts got headlines in the papers. Bad publicity was better than no publicity at all.

Frances was running short of selfless zeal. Before it ran out, she was obliged to search the house. There were two rooms left to check on the second floor, the extra bath and Madeline's book-lined study. There was no one in the tub behind the shower curtain. There was nobody sprawled across the knee-hole desk. The closet was crammed with papers and filing boxes. Some fell on her head. She did not pick them up. She started to climb the stairs to the third-floor landing. As she reached the highest stair, all hell broke loose. In fact, hell had been tuning up for several seconds, coinciding with the rain of boxes from the closet shelves.

From one of the guest rooms came a grisly din. In a wooden house, the din would have shaken the rafters. Pieces of furniture were sliding and colliding. Were mirrors or windows popping out of their frames? Was a bird caught inside that made this frantic flapping? A very large bird, the size of a Western condor? Frances heard another crash and a nameless clanging. She could hear them in the pit of her stomach and the soles of her feet. Madeline had threatened suicide, not murder. Suicide was a sedentary venture. Someone who had taken pills was limp and feeble, too weak to be the agent of that clamor.

Frances was brave enough to hunt for corpses. She did not want to tangle with animate malefactors. They, or he, had a heavy tread. Was he wearing boots? Were they kicking the chairs to pieces, or each other? Why would a pack of thieves smash up the guest room? Madeline's silver was stored in a chest in the pantry. Frances crouched down and tried to plug her ears. Thieves, like suicides, plied their trade in silence. They did not call attention to their deeds by screaming, at a pitch that was rarely reached by human lungs. Frances backed down two steps and froze in place. What if the screams were made by nothing living? What if the house was beset by noisy ghosts, haunting the spot where Madeline had met her doom? Poltergeists sometimes camped in a single chamber; more often they usurped whole households, room by room. Poltergeists made bad landlords for human tenants. They harassed their tenants, plotting their eviction. They hoisted them up and shook them in unseen fists; they stuck out an unseen foot and sent them sprawling. They made floorboards move like a rubber conveyor belt. They enjoyed sending streams of blood gushing down the staircase.

Frances was poised for flight when she heard a shout, a masculine bellow followed by a female shriek. Poltergeists were good at faking human voices. She noticed, as she listened, that their language was quite profane. She wondered how they had learned such modern swearwords. Was "ball-breaker" a term that was known to ancient ghosts? Or did Frances put ghosts, incorrectly, into period costume? She heard a spate of words that began with f. The voices were familiar now. PolterPaul and PolterMadeline.

Frances jumped to her feet in anger and kicked the stair rail. She ran to the room that housed the fracas and kicked the door. She kicked again. The medley of howls grew louder. To the uproar was added the sound of running water. Frances hopped on one foot. Her toes hurt. The pain helped to clear her head. It was just as painful to discover she had been a patsy. Madeline never took pills. She had the gagging reflex. She did not even eat chewy foods for fear of choking. Paul and Madeline were co-producing a steamy drama. They were at loggerheads about the dénouement. Madeline wanted a romantic resolution. She had used threats of pills to expedite that plotline. Paul did not want the lovers wed by final curtain. He had decided to triangulate the action. If he brought on another character—i.e., Frances—she could step in and throw the plot off course. If Paul had offered her a starring role, she might have taken it. She had no inclination to play the second lead. She did not want to watch a preview or a performance. Left to herself, she would not have purchased seats.

Frances stood at the guest-room door massaging her foot. The ruckus inside had dwindled to a murmur. An amorous murmur, marked by suggestive laughter. The water stopped running. Perhaps they had climbed into the tub. If they started to fight in the bathtub, Paul might drown her. Or she might drown Paul. With luck, they might drown each other. Frances had earned her lifesaving badge at camp. They would not get the benefit of her special knowledge. Should she let them drown, or burst in and surprise them? Which would hurt worse, death or humiliation? People who had their taste for flagrant conduct would not feel disgraced by being caught in action. They would laugh at Frances and flaunt their lumps and bruises. And what if she opened the door on the Scene of Scenes? Would they ask her to join them, or grind away unmindful? One thing was certain with pigs like Paul and Madeline: They would not try to save her face or spare her feelings.

Hypocritical Frances. Her heart was black as coal. She had worked herself into a fine-haired righteous swivet. She had censured Paul and Madeline for lust and excess, and considered doing excessive things with Paul. There was no health in her; she had coveted her landlady's beau. Worse still, she had imagined that he might covet her. Who would covet a lowly worm, however tow-haired? A worm should be seen, not heard. A worm conforms. Frances had tried to rise above her station. She had tried to borrow spirit and height from Paul. She might never reach his height in her only lifetime. Paul Treat was an artist, and Frances Girard was a clerk.

Frances climbed Madeline's stairs to Madeline's garret. She emptied Madeline's closet and Madeline's drawers. She vacuumed Madeline's rugs and dusted her furniture. She mopped her floors and waxed her kitchen linoleum. She stripped the bed and folded Madeline's sheets. She put the sheets in the hamper with Madeline's towels. She packed her own belongings in a suitcase. The suitcase had been a hand-me-down from Madeline. She wrote a check for the rent, but she left no note. She propped the check on the mantelpiece, in plain view. Her winter coat took up too much room in the suitcase. She decided to wear it, as well as her fur-lined boots.

The suitcase was heavy. She slid it as far as the landing. She bumped it down the first flight of stairs and paused at the guest room. She listened at the guest-room door. Paul and Madeline were quiet. Had they left the house, alerted by the roar of the Hoover? Or were they lying in bed, sleeping the sleep of the sated? Frances had been packing and cleaning for an hour and a half. In that interval a couple might have joined and rejoined six times. Sliding and bumping, Frances carried her bag two more flights. She got out her key ring and pulled off Madeline's house keys. She left them in a bowl on the table with the morning mail. She stepped outside. She closed Madeline's front door behind her. The weather was hot. It was more like August than June. People would stare at Frances in her coat and boots. She deserved their stares. She deserved their smiles and jeers. She deserved to walk thirty blocks carrying her suitcase, passing by buses waiting for the light at bus stops, ignoring the empty taxis that slowed down and honked. She deserved the blisters on her heels and the cramps in her hands, and the spots in front of her eyes from the glaring heat. In fact, her penance was lighter than she deserved. She should have had bigger blisters and sharper cramps.

Edie Childs asked no questions when Frances arrived at her door. She put Frances to bed in a cool, dim room with the blinds drawn. She brought her cold water and told her to sip it slowly. She sponged her forehead with a washcloth soaked in cologne. Frances slept like a stone between linen sheets smooth with age. The next morning, Edie brought her her favorite breakfast on a tray: coffee with boiled milk and an egg fried as stiff as a wallet. When Frances tried to get up, Edie pressed her down. Frances slept through the day and dreamed no dreams worth recording. Once she heard Edie hushing Hill Childs when he talked too loudly. In the evening, Edie woke her with soup and crackers for supper, and the news that she had found her an apartment. A colleague of Hill's had been sent for a year to Denmark. The apartment, which was furnished, came with a black-and-white cat. Edie unfolded an enormous damask napkin and tucked it over Frances's collar, like a bib. "Your problems are solved," she said as she straightened the covers. "Now you can have your little collapse in peace."

Frances was as weak as any convalescent. She followed orders and stayed in bed all weekend. She dozed and read and listened to the life of the household: early meals, church on Sunday, and sherry after the service. There was much to be said for an orderly, well-run household. Frances's life could be orderly, too, if run by Edie. With Edie in charge, her life could be as peaceful as a sickroom. Soon Edie would submit a bill for private nursing, and Frances would return it, stamped and paid in full. The payment would consist of: the story of Madeline's "suicide" (reported in minutest detail, many times over); a season of Saturday lunches and daily phone calls; and dinners with friends of Hill's who were still unwed. Edie's yoke was heavy; Paul's would have been no easier. With Edie, Frances knew where the harness pinched. She adjusted her pace to keep the weight evenly balanced. Paul's pace was too fast. His frame was built for distance. Fastened to Paul, would she not grow lame and footsore? Fastened to Edie, however, her limbs might wither. Living by Edie's code, she lived a worm's life. Who, or what, could she be had she kept in step with Paul? Paul saw through her, where Edie saw her own reflection. What had Paul seen—someone bold, inspired, and restless? Someone lonely and gifted, whose gifts, once uncovered, might prosper? With Paul in the lead, her stride might have lengthened and quickened. If Paul had prevailed, the worm might well have turned.

Frances had found a new beau, who was also an author. He had
won the Harwood Prize for Younger Poets. He was thin, as a
poet should be, and had insomnia. He subsisted on nuts and
fruit, like the creatures of the field. He was gentle and good and
shy of other people. He built bookshelves for Frances's apartment and painted them himself. He enjoyed taking walks. He
enjoyed staring out of the window. When he stayed overnight,
he kept to his side of the bed. Sometimes Frances woke up and
found him at the kitchen table, writing down lines that had
come to him as he lay sleepless. He wrote very slowly. He
scratched out as much as he wrote. There were days when he
labored, hunched over, to find one right word. Edie approved of
her poet, who had lovely manners, and remembered to put on
socks when he came for dinner. Frances admired him and
found his companionship restful. Even when he was working,
he took up so little space. He would bring her his poems and ask
her permission to read them. He read standing up, while Frances stretched out on the couch. His poems were simple. They
were set in a rough, northern landscape, at three seasons of the
year—he never wrote about summer. There were birds in his
poems, and plants, but very few people. If people were introduced, they were harming creation, setting fires, cutting trees, or
diverting streams and rivers. Frances listened with attention.
With closed eyes, she could listen better. She liked the poems,
but at times they made her peevish. She would long for some
drama, color, riot, or magic. Why didn't they flash on and off or
glow in the dark? Why couldn't they walk on stilts, or bark like
seals? Why weren't they painted like a rainbow, or wired for
sound? It wasn't the fault of her kindly, serious poet. The fault
was Paul Treat's; he had spoiled her for peaceful scenes.

Several months later her poet departed for Iowa, leaving nothing behind him except for his well-crafted bookshelves. He promised to send her a poem about their alliance. When he did, its central image was sooty snowdrifts. There was snow on the sidewalks to go with the snow in the poem. The pavements were scorching when Frances had last seen Paul Treat. Through the cold and the sleet, Frances went to the Mercer Place Theatre where *A Midsummer Night's Dream* was still playing to boisterous audiences. She waited outside the stage door when the curtain went down. Sometimes she sat through the play, all five acts and nine scenes. Very soon she would catch sight of Paul. He might notice her first. She had made no fixed plan and had memorized no prepared speech. She was taking a risk in defiance of sense and tranquillity. Would he run to her side or pass by without deigning to greet her? Was she equal to losing him? What would she do if she found him? She asked these vexed questions while making her way to the lobby, where a crowd was forgathering to stretch their legs during intermission. Did that man up the aisle by the doors, who was turning her way, have Paul's height and Paul's beard? Or perhaps he was thinner and taller? In case it was Paul, she took cover behind a fat woman. She peeked over the woman's fur collar. Paul had already seen her. She was sunk. She was saved. Paul was striding remorselessly toward her. He swept down the aisle, scattering his public like pigeons. Frances took a step back, crushing somebody's toes with her heel. With the houselights full up, Paul reached out his arms and engulfed her.

II
GROUP SEX

Frances and Paul were arguing over the source of Pom Foster's nickname.

"It's from *Winnie-the-Pooh,*" said Frances. "'The more it snows, tiddely-pom, the more it goes, tiddely-pom, on snowing.'"

Paul had decided that Pom was baby talk for Pamela. Frances was holding out for A. A. Milne. They were two hours southwest of Boston, clearing Hartford on Route 91, after the champagne christening of Pom and Toby Foster's baby, Joshua. They had left the party early because Frances had seen pure evil in Paul's blue eyes. She knew that look. Once, at a hamburger palace called The Hippo, they sat waiting twenty minutes for some service. Suddenly, Paul had bellowed like the restaurant's wild namesake. The owner, the manager, and two waitresses came running, but that had not made up, to Frances, for the stares and whispers and hasty exits.

"That's Wasp Heaven up there," said Frances, propping her feet against the glove compartment. She had taken off her shoes because Paul didn't want the black paint scratched, but left on her socks because bare feet made greasy toe prints.

"Blond parents, blond babies, blond dogs. Did I ever tell you my favorite thing from *Vogue?* 'Why don't you rinse your blond children's hair in dead champagne, as the French do?'"

"Why don't you rinse your dead children's hair in blond champagne?" said Paul, and snorted like a hog.

Paul steered with his left thumb or his right knee. At the moment, no part of his person was in contact with the wheel, and they were passing a fuel truck.

"Barney Oldfield," said Frances, instead of grabbing the wheel. Paul ignored her.

"Wasp Heaven is funny, coming from you," he said.

Frances relaxed; he was driving with both thumbs now.

"I have no roots. We moved around too much." She tilted her chin. "Girard isn't Anglo-Saxon anyway; it's Huguenot."

Frances was only a closet pariah, but Paul was the real thing. Nothing attracted Frances like the scorned visionary, the proud pauper, the embattled artist. "I go down for artists," she had been known to say, perfectly aware of the contradiction between her classic profile and her low talk. Paul had begun to write plays, or, rather, he mimeographed sheets of notation for his actors to improvise on, and kept encoded logbooks charting the development of the improvisations during rehearsals. Critics and arts-council officers came to these rehearsals, and waited in suspense for the awesome moment when work-in-progress would crystallize into work of art. Their suspense was protracted, since Paul's current work, based on the incest taboo throughout the ages, had been in progress for almost a year. Snippy articles began appearing in drama reviews and trade newspapers. Paul answered every one in a serial statement blaming the death of the theatre on the stranglehold of the written word. Paul was a storm center, and took to carrying himself like the captain of a gale-tossed ship. With his vast brow, impressive stature, and auburn hair, anonymity ranked very low on his list of fears.

Frances was in love with anonymity. Her myopia was protection on city streets. She could not recognize acquaintances half a block away, and always supposed they did not see her either. If she passed a man she had met the night before at a party, she never tried to stop and greet him, since she assumed he would not remember her name or face. Her profession, as an editor of books, gave her a podium for her views on self-effacement. She disapproved of colleagues who used the phrase "my author." (Sometimes she even heard them say "my book.") These glory boys would grab a writer's coattails and forget they were only toadies and hangers-on. At most, an editor was like a teacher whose joy should be in getting the best from the student, and who must expect no fame or credit in this life.

Frances didn't bray these notions to the winds; she saved them for her monthly lunch with Toby Foster, who was with the Boston office of the Harwood Press. She might begin the litany: "Editors are service people. . . ." "Bostonians think Harvard professors are their children's tutors," he might answer in his patient, intimate drawl. After this promising start, they could take on lawyers and stockbrokers, who wouldn't admit to the service rule, and accountants, whose only virtue was that they did. These shared pieties were the basis of their friendship. It mattered also that Toby's mother knew her father; they had grown up together in Cincinnati. Alone in the East, except for Edie and well-lost Madeline, Toby knew who she was and whom she came from. Frances left lunches with Toby giddy with high-mindedness; the air was purer around their table, but thin to breathe.

At the Fosters' house, however, the air was charged. Frances stayed there on her business trips to Boston. She and Toby administered Harwood's annual prize for college poets. Pom took Frances right over; it was Girls Together. She had to follow Pom as she chugged around the house. "I have an energy prob-

lem," Pom had announced, dumping cream cheese onto a plate
out of a heart-shaped wicker basket. Pom was modest. Four
new projects were an average for her day—making coeur à la
crème; tailoring a suit for Toby; building chairs from a photo-
graph in *Good Design;* inventing a new method for teaching
Spanish to backward readers. These projects were ranged
around the house like the Stations of the Cross. Some would be
finished and some would not; the undertaking was all. Frances's
head swam and her legs felt like macaroni, symptoms she only
got roaming department stores or museums.

Paul began to growl, a low rasp in the back of his throat. In their
private language this sound was called The Natives Are Restless. He looked at Frances as if he would like to bite her.

"You don't share the driving," he said.

It was true. She borrowed no power from being behind the
wheel. She didn't like steering shopping carts at the market,
either. She decided to placate him with a little malice.

"Pom has fits," she said. "She just falls to the floor. Toby
stands over her and won't even pick her up."

"She's a hysteric," said Paul, "and he's a faggot."

"She does dream in Technicolor," agreed Frances. "She also
sees animals in the back of the car."

"Bullshit," said Paul, but his ears were pricking up. "What
kind of animals?"

"I don't know, but she was driving to Needham, where she
teaches, and she could see them in the rearview mirror. They
followed her into the ladies' room at school."

"I hope they ate her," said Paul. "I'd like to eat her."

"You're an outrage," Frances said, laughing; she had not
quite come to terms with this kind of talk.

Frances was a sponge for technical language. Osmotically she had picked up the jargons of surfers, fly-fishermen, truckers, and sound-studio engineers. Before Paul, her profanity had been grade-school level. Half the time she didn't know what the odd words meant. She tried a few of Paul's choice ones out on Toby, who told her never to use expressions ending in "job" or "off." Bad language was a part of Paul's self-made image; some of it was theatre talk, and some of it he had lifted from *Ulysses*. Frances copied it because it lined her up with artists and outcasts.

Then why did Paul's lewd remarks still stir her fears? She treasured his impish nature and his choice obscenities. But language was never just fancy dress or borrowed feathers; it might reflect the inner imp, and his real desires. Perhaps he really wanted to perform vile acts with Pom. Pom was small and taut, like a well-made pony, with strong legs, and a perfect, rounded crupper. Her streaky hair looked chopped, not trimmed, and some piece of her clothing was always unpressed or unbuttoned. She arched her chest when she was talking to men, or women. She also stroked her neck and scratched her knees. Every gesture she made was jerky and urgent. Frances had swallowed an image taken from fashion journals, that sexual signals can only be transmitted by the graceful and well groomed. She did not like being wary of Pom, but now that she'd started, she remembered Pom bragging about propositions from the Wards and the De Lessières. On the other hand, Pom was known for her tabloid mind.

Paul was tailgating a Lincoln, and honking hard.

"It's a blue-hair," said Frances, leaning forward. "Don't honk. You'll scare her. She'll slow way down."

He forced the Lincoln over to the right and sped ahead.

"Seventy-five?" she asked. "There's a lot of traffic."

He flung his hands off the wheel and Frances shrieked. Then he eased down to sixty, laughing like a fiend from hell. Frances was phobic on the road, and Paul was a tease. She pushed her fists into her lap and prayed she wouldn't comment next time. They stopped for dinner at a Hoof 'n' Claw outside of Bridgeport. They ordered little rock lobster tails, which tasted of iodine. Paul had finished two dinners, five beers, and a cup of coffee. Frances was spooning damp frozen chives on a baked potato. She could tell his mind was wandering; he was taking his pulse.

"You inhale your food," she said, dipping into the sour-cream substitute.

He looked hurt. "Slow eaters are passive-aggressive."

Without unclasping his fingers from his wrist, he pushed his back against the side partition and slung his legs up on the leather banquette. His feet stuck way out into the aisle.

"This booth is too small," he grumbled.

Frances felt her stomach knot up and little veins began to drum in her temples. Just once it would be nice to relax and linger at the table. She liked to sip and ruminate; he liked to bolt and wolf. If she wanted to finish her meal, she would have to distract him.

"You are aware," she said, dressing her salad, "that Pom Foster was molested by her choirmaster."

"No," breathed Paul. He was enraptured.

"On two separate occasions," said Frances cagily. "She got him unfrocked."

"Where?" asked Paul.

"In Vermont, where she comes from," answered Frances.

"No—where on her?"

"I didn't ask, for Lord's sake!"

"You never get the good stuff," growled Paul unjustly.

"I do so. I tell you everything!"

"Skittish broads like that are all talk," said Paul. "Put your tongue in her ear and she calls the National Guard."

Frances looked up, startled. Paul was sounding very knowledgeable. She knew he was a great student of the unconscious, however, and dedicated to the sexual origin of all behavior. Every one of his rehearsals started with a dream clinic. She could imagine his actors sleeping at night with their faces screwed up, frowning, trying hard to make dreams for the director, the way cats catch locusts to drop at their masters' feet.

A waitress was steering the dessert wagon down their aisle. Frances hailed her and took a piece of Nesselrode pie. Paul's eyes were still glazed and thoughtful. She could spin enough tales to see her through pie and coffee.

Paul had forgotten to shut the windows in his loft before they left. Frances went over to check the sills for built-up soot. She picked up a dirty sock and wiped off the surfaces. Then she went into the bathroom to inspect the floor. She put back all the tiny hexagonal tiles that had come out of their slots. She moistened a paper tissue with spit and began to rub at the water marks on the mirror.

Paul appeared in the doorway. "If you're cleaning with saliva again, I'll kill you!"

She squealed but she kept on rubbing. Paul had various crotchets, but this one she disregarded. Once she had reached for his chocolate ice-cream cone to take a lick. He had howled with rage and pushed her away so she stumbled. That was how she had learned that he never shared milk products. She might lunge at his yogurt cup with her spoon now and then, just to tease him, but she was careful not to test him any further.

Paul's kitchen was hidden inside a closet. He opened the ice-box and took out a bottle of cola. He banged some ice off the freezer coils with a knife and filled two glasses. Frances took hers plain; he cut a section of lime for himself.

"Now," said Paul as he handed Frances her drink. "The De Lessières are French hotshots who write children's books. Who are the Wards?"

He was back to their conversation at the end of dinner. He had been so unresponsive that she'd thought he was blocking new scenes in his head. She should have known him better. The story was much too spicy.

"The De Lessières are rich," said Frances, pushing the lamp table into neater alignment with the armchair. "They have one of those French houses where everything is done in the same pattern. You know, the walls match the bedspread matches the rug matches the slipcovers."

"Move it or lose it," said Paul. "You're like a Shakespearean messenger."

"I am trying to explain," emphasized Frances, "that Pom is a disgusting snob. She also has a perfect ear. You can always tell when the De Lessières are in from Paris. Pom can't ask if you've seen *Claire's Knee;* she has to say 'Have you seen *Le Genou de Claire?*'"

"I'm going to bite you," warned Paul.

Frances loved to keep him in suspense. It was the only time that the balance of power shifted her way.

Then she relented. She shrugged her shoulders. "The Wards are nobody special. They were graduate students in the M.A. program with Toby."

"Are those the only two couples, or were there more?"

She got edgy. "Why? Do you want to be put on the sign-up sheet?"

"Come on, Frances. I need to know for my art."

She relaxed. She could handle that explanation. Paul was as inquisitive as an ape, but in a higher cause. She was curious, too, but she thought Pom's boasts were a figment. For one thing, Frances couldn't imagine the dialogue. How were these civilized solicitations put into language?

"O.K., let's do it," said Paul. He had closed his eyes. "I'm Jean-Loup, or that egghead Ward, and I'm pressing up against you in the corridor."

"Don't ask me," said Frances, who was plumping up the pillows on the bed. "I mean, where was Toby? And where was Grisette, or whatever her name is?"

"You are never still," said Paul. "Sit down or I'll knock you down."

Frances slid to the floor and sat cross-legged in front of his chair.

"You're right," she went on. "It's not logical. Jean-Loup should say 'Meet me for lunch,' or 'Here is the key to my garçonnière.' Why drag in the others?"

"'Why' is easy." Paul became very grave. "The dramatic moment lies in 'how.'"

"Nothing is wrong between sixteen people who love each other?" Frances killed herself laughing. She fell over on her side and shook with laughter.

Paul refused to take part. He nudged her flank end with the toe of his shoe. Then he nudged harder.

"Pay attention," he ordered. "I want this solved."

She just lay there, giggling and snorting. "I don't want to anymore. I'm sick of the Fosters. I'd rather do the rape in Scene Four."

Frances had made a most unwise decision. She was used to being a laboratory animal, but the last time they had explored the rape it had ended badly. As part of the incest spectrum in his play, Paul needed to include the drunken father and the pubescent daughter. One out of every twenty girls, he had read, is forced by a close male relative. It was a brand-new scene, and Paul had not thought it out fully. This was the only acting school Frances would ever attend, so she was eager to get high marks.

Paul had put her down on the couch. "You're asleep, he wakes you up. You think he's come to kiss you goodnight, you see he's drunk. You get scared, and you resist. The thing to remember is, don't let him," Paul had instructed. "Do anything—use your nails, teeth, fists, anything, but don't let him."

"He's my father," objected Frances, sitting back up. "I'd be in shock. How could I fight?"

Paul put his palm flat on her chest and pushed her down again. He set a pillow under her head and covered her with a jacket.

"Let's do it my way now," he said. "We'll try it your way some other time."

He closed the shutters and turned off the lamp. Then he went into the bathroom and stationed himself behind the door.

Father/Paul had advanced or sneaked to the edge of the bed/couch. Daughter/Frances gave a yelp when she felt his breath on her cheek. She remembered her cue, and raised her arms for the good-night kiss. Father/Paul pulled her into his arms and reached back for her skirt. He pulled up her skirt. He started kneading her rump. She was pinned in so tight that her arms stuck out like two sticks. She could bend them partway, at the elbow, but not enough to land a solid blow. Her face was smashed into his chest. One of his buttons bit into her forehead, right on her chicken-pox scar. Father's/Paul's hands stopped working for the space of a second. She heard a sharp report, like cloth ripping, and flew right out of character. She began to protest, and found she could not move her mouth. She could not form words; she could only raise a loud angry buzz. Father/Paul, still deep in his role, was kneading and laughing. She lost her head. He was going too far. She could not breathe; she was choking, or thought she was. In panic she pitched herself backward, and broke his grasp. She lay gasping and sobbing wildly, flailing her feet. He moved over, crossed his legs, and sat there watching her. She did not like the look of his eyes; there seemed to be a film over them. Then he blinked twice, uncrossed his legs, and stretched his back.

"Calm down," he said, yawning. "It wasn't a failure. I can use parts of it."

Frances gulped. Her mouth hung open in surprise. Paul had thought that she was asking him a question.

"Yeah," he answered. "That's one way to play it, where he doesn't finish. You did good," he added, and reached over to pat her hand.

He had not noticed that her collapse was real, or had just ignored it. Either way, he had not treated her like an amateur. In retrospect, Frances felt she could be proud of herself. Her memory was short, but the memory was heady. By now she saw these improvisations as tests of courage.

She got up and stood in front of his chair, a recruit at attention.

"Can we start now, please?" she asked. "I need time later to finish indexing the self-hypnosis book."

"You always want your own way." He shook his fist at her. "I'm still on the Fosters. I don't like breaking set that fast."

He was arguing for form's sake, and Frances knew it. Already he was capitulating; he was reaching into his back pocket for a miniature memo pad. He began flipping through the pages. He jotted down ideas on tiny memo pads in a code of glyphs. He had been refining this picture-writing since he had learned to write. The key to the code was deposited in his bank box. He wanted his biographers to have access to his notebooks, but not other playwrights, who were larcenists of ideas. For this reason he also kept his back pocket buttoned.

"All right," said Paul. "Last time we did it with you resisting."

"To the end," said Frances. "I'm a game girl, aren't I?"

"This will be easier and shorter," he said. "You just act dead."

"Dead when?" asked Frances. "After the good-night kiss?"

"No kiss," said Paul. "He gets it in while you're still asleep. Here. Take off your clothes and put on this shirt. Pretend it's a nightgown."

Frances began unbuttoning, unzipping, and untying. Her bare skin burned and shrank, as if she were stripping in front of strangers. Covered, she felt better. Paul's shirt was as long on her as a clergyman's cassock.

"Are you ready?" asked Paul. "You can't cop out in the middle."

"I'm O.K. Just as long as you don't cut off my breath."

This time she got into the bed and lay on her back.

"No," said Paul. She opened her eyes. "Lie on your stomach and face stage right. He'll be coming at you from stage left. It's more powerful if he turns you over. Come on. Let's do it."

She turned onto her stomach. She could hear Paul moving around, darkening the room. There was no light coming from anywhere, not even from underneath the blinds. There was a lump of hot lead in her stomach. A trail of ants was progressing up her thighs. They were rounding the tops of her buttocks, where there should be no nerve ends. A good actress would be counting and emptying her mind, or relaxing the segments of her body one by one. Or thinking dead thoughts and conjuring up dead images: eyeless statues, blasted stumps, quilted satin, banks of clouds, sheets of rain. Frances was tense, not limp. She did not feel dead at all; she was feeling flayed.

She heard a skitter, like a rat across the floor. Then a creak— surely a weight lifting off the chair springs. The bed gave, it was a knee pressing down on the mattress. She clawed the sheets to stop her body from sliding. Any second his hand would land upon her shoulder.

She opened her eyes halfway. What made the room so black? If this were a normal rehearsal, there would be work lights on the stage and in the hall. The lights were required by law, to prevent injuries to actors or crew. She was outside the reach of union regulations. There was no foreman from the actors' guild to voice her rights. Paul had been up before the guild that year already, on charges of exploitation. He had kept little Josey Ware going over the same long monologue for twelve straight hours. Someone had called her husband, who dragged her off the stage and carried her home. The incident had been smoothed over, and she was back on the show five days later. Paul had shrugged it off. Josey's work was much improved. "I had to break her down to help her break through." He had more confidence in means-end arguments than Joseph Stalin. Frances's reaction had been partisan and derisive. "Actors' rights," she had jeered. "Actors are children. You know their needs better than they do. They're lucky to have you!"

Now, for failing in charity, for sitting in the seat of the scornful, and for siding with Management, Frances would be punished. She was comforted to think so, at least, since it gave her a reason for lying face down on Paul's bed, wearing Paul's shirt, in his pitch-black room, waiting to be raped, when every other reason had deserted her.

The rape was on, and there was no saying "Oh, it's just old Paul, that big old bear, furry old funny old Paul, cries in movies, won't share milk products, locks the car doors going through Harlem, Paul's a screech, he's the universal Id, who but old Paul . . ." It didn't work. He was someone else. He was Dr. Strangerod.

This person, who had turned her on her back, was working at her limbs and chest with flat, splayed palms; and Paul was as deft and steady as a fly-caster. He had left wet smears on her face; and Paul never slobbered. He pushed her legs apart at right angles, and set his knees on her thighs to hold them down. He started driving at her soft closed flesh. Whales have bones, and men do not, but he was as hard as wood. Her brain was dim, like the brain of a fish, and she tried to think. *This could not happen in any theatre; there are laws and censors.* She dimmed out now, and fought back weakly to the surface. She saw some hope there, like a shaft of light through the blinds. *He can't do this on stage, so he will have to stop. He will rehearse to the brink; he won't go over. He has his marginal attention, his internal monitor; he says actors who lose themselves in their parts are just like lunatics. . . .*

Still he drove and he thrust; she was lashed to a machine. She could hear strange grunts, and Paul was always still and seemly. *This is a rape, the same as in an alley. . . .*

She felt a thud, which bounced her on the mattress. It was the impact of a fist pounding down on the bed beside her. Her thighs were free, but she found that it hurt to move them. She heard a crash, like an object breaking against the wall.

"I can't get in! You closed up like a clam! You locked me out!"

It was Paul's own voice. When the light switched on, she could see it was Paul's own form, towering over the bed in a kind of majestic snit. But peevishness is fearful in a person of such large size. When she asked to leave a movie in the middle, he could look like that, or when she had a date for dinner with a friend on a night when he wanted her to take rehearsal notes. Once he had seen the cat on her bed and he had yelled like that. The cat was lying on top of her pillow, curled in a circle. "You let that cat drag his anus on the sheets? I'm not sleeping in there!" They had driven back downtown to his loft, at three in the morning. Now he never spent the night in her apartment unless she changed the bedclothes right in front of him and locked the cat in the bathroom until they got up for breakfast the next morning.

Paul stopped towering, and began to hover anxiously.

"What's the matter? You look awful. You've lost your color."

He rubbed her cheek. She brought her knees very slowly to her chest and rolled over on one side, facing away from him. She felt bleak and empty, like the surface of the moon. She wanted to burrow her head in the pillow and sleep it off. Paul did not like it when Frances was silent and inert. It scared him. It put his universe out of whack. He wanted her up and hopping, so he poked her shoulder.

"Come on, little chicken, on your feet; nobody loves a dead person."

He poked again, and shook the shoulder for good measure.

"Do you hear me? You need a hamburger. I'll take you to Cullinan's. God damn it, Frances, if you're sick I'm going to kill you!" He bent down and pulled back her eyelid, looking for signs of life.

Frances gave up. She had enough strength to fasten her teeth onto his wrist, but not to bite down. She did not have enough strength to resist the move to Cullinan's, although she hated an actors' bar. Models named Ingrid with heart-shaped mouths would beg Pete Cullinan for introductions to Paul, because they had notions about breaking into acting and had heard that Paul sometimes used amateurs and beginners. That was true; Paul liked to mold an actor early, the way the Jesuits like to take on a child before it is seven.

Frances let Paul stand her up. He dropped her skirt over her head and zipped up the waist, a little off center. He stuffed her arms into the sleeves of her shirt, but he made her button it. He was too impatient. It was midnight. The action at Cullinan's had been under way for almost an hour.

Paul got out his comb and took a few swipes at her rumpled hair.

"All right, little waif, I've got you in shape. Now we have to hustle."

They rode uptown in a cab. When he wasn't taking his pulse, Paul was making notes. They were an agenda for a meeting with a rich young show-business lawyer, who might or might not be at Cullinan's that night, and might or might not be persuaded to kick in some funds for the incest play, which ate money the way a secondhand Cadillac eats gas.

Frances let her head fall hard against the seatback, in a position portraying extreme fatigue and weakness. Her weakness was more the result of shame than of muscles strained in the course of the rape improv. Her body was tired, but her mind would not let her rest. *I am an underground person, I am a worm, I am less than a flea. I have no fight; all girls should take contact sports in school. I want to go home; the hypnosis index is due. I am like a sheep. I am a set of tracks to roll over. No. I'm the roadbed. I want to see Toby. Toby is my only male friend. He sent me that thing on the retreat house; I wonder if they take girl pilgrims. I want to live in silence, with kindly nuns. . . .*

"I can't," said Frances, out loud to Paul. "I feel like a piece of Swiss cheese."

"Oh, no?" he said. "Baby, that's your lookout."

They stopped for the light near the corner of Forty-fourth. She could see Cullinan's green awning down the side street. Paul leaned forward and told the driver her address.

"I'm getting out," he said. "You're making a big mistake."

She gave a sweet, sad smile, like the youthful Lillian Gish. She was smiling at his back, however. He had slammed the door. Paul had two main voices, one for pleading and one for threats. Tonight he was threatening ingénues and the hardening of his heart. Frances was punchy from threats. She thought of St. Sebastian. Another arrow, to him, more or less, must have been all the same.

Even worms and fleas have an instinct for self-protection. Frances spent the next three days working at home, ignoring the phone. She asked her secretary to cancel her appointments, and to tell callers she was down South with an author on a publicity tour. She had to put herself out of touch, because Paul was a bird dog. She had hidden out once before and he had bribed the doorman, who let him into her apartment with a duplicate set of keys. When he was in a hurry, and her telephone rang busy, he would tell the operator there had been a death in the family, and break in on her call. If he suspected she was not down South, he might watch her building. As it was, she went out for groceries after dark, when he was at the theatre, wearing a kerchief over her hair and a raincoat that was much too big on her. This bit of intrigue added zest to her retreat. She spread her index cards in rows upon the rug, and spent the days happily shifting around on her hands and knees. She loved her job, and even found virtue in the donkeywork.

By the end of the third day, she was restless nonetheless. She wanted to give Paul a healthy jolt; she did not want to lose him. She decided to answer the phone, but it would not ring.

The doorbell rang instead, and then again. Someone was pounding the door, which rattled on its hinges.

Paul stood there. He threw his arms wide open. She ran to him and he lifted her off her feet.

"Little creature," he said, "don't despise your poor bad animal."

"You forget how large and you hurt me." She sobbed, and clung to his waist.

"Look. David and Goliath." He turned her toward the mirror. "Maybe we are mismatched."

"I'm your sidekick dwarf," laughed Frances, and he squeezed her harder. Between weeping and laughing she got her spirits back. By the time she was restored, there was a large wet patch on Paul's shirtfront.

"Oh, Lord," she said contritely. "Do you want me to get my hair dryer?"

"No, leave it," said Paul. "You drool when you're happy, too."

"How did you know I was here?"

"I pestered Ruthanne till she told me."

"I'll get her," said Frances.

"No, you won't," said Paul. "She held out on me for three whole days. She was pretty tough."

Paul was late for the theatre. When he left, Frances tried to go back to work. She kept sitting down and stopping, or getting sidetracked by lint and cat hairs on the rug. She felt addled and lighthearted; her mind was scattered all over the room, like her index cards. For one moment she mourned the loss of her concentration, and the shape and silence of her abbreviated retreat. Paul had planted her feet back on the high road to adventure.

Left to herself, she would have stuck to the side roads. She was Sancho Panza; this phase of her destiny was to be lived out as a straight man.

The windows in Toby's office looked out over the Charles River. It was a privileged view, for Toby was a senior editor. He was emeritus before his time, a kind of resident scholar. He had turned down the more visible post of editor-in-chief. "I hate budgets and personnel," he had said to Frances. "And besides I'd have to keep my door open."

The staff at Harwood had learned to approach Toby's office on tiptoe. They never marched up and knocked on his door; they hovered, and tapped. Frances had even heard Albion Harwood, the president, whispering to an English publisher, "That's Toby Foster's door; he does our Double Dome books." Publishers revere academics, and Toby dealt with professors. If he could talk to them, his colleagues reasoned, he must be their peer and rival. Hammy Griner, the editor-in-chief, apologized to Toby for every Harwood book on the best-seller list. Hammy was round and whiskery. He would hunch his shoulders forward and duck his head, reducing himself in physical stature as if to portray his distance from Toby's intellectual standards. Toby did nothing to check the course of Hammy's self-abasement. He would stand two feet away, the distance he chose for any close encounter, and let Hammy tie himself in knots and run on like a louver-door salesman. Hammy would break down, molecule by molecule, while Toby's contours would grow sharper and sharper, like Percival about to lay hands on the Grail. Frances hated to see it. She had sometimes intervened, lifted Hammy off his knees, walked him back to his office, and restored him with coffee and book chat.

It was not Toby's fault. He believed in the life of the mind. He did not see other people except as containers of ideas. Frances hardly minded; he tuned her in and out all the time. "Small talk is fine," he liked to say, "but we have to remember it's small." Toby was restful to be with, for a man. He didn't like to touch, to emphasize a point, or to express affection. He didn't flirt, unless he was flirting when his drawl got more pronounced. Frances never felt like prey around Toby, and assumed he lacked the predatory instinct. She wondered, at times, about Pom and her whipstitch energies; she remembered the two blond babies, and the picture fell into place. She thought Toby might be that rare Christian man for whom marriage was an ethical laboratory.

Paul was suspicious of Frances's accounts of Toby. "Those simon-pure types are cesspools," he said. She would frown, but she didn't answer back. In fact, Frances had dug a pit in her excellent memory. Into the pit she had dropped Toby's sexual gossip, and his jokes about cabbage leaves and nose flutes, and covered it over with sod and sticks, like a bear trap. Now and then he would make another blue remark, and she would plunge down the pit, like the bear, and remember that he had this sixth-grade tendency. He looked like a grown-up altar boy, and she appointed herself chief curator of that image.

They were sitting across from each other at Toby's kneehole desk, trading entries for the college poetry contest. There were more than a hundred poems. So far, only two had reached the semifinals. If they both liked a poem, they would stop to read it aloud.

"Here's a little number called *Dominatrix*."

Toby handed Frances a coffee-colored sheet of stationery. Frances flinched. Somehow his face had widened and flattened. The Pale Loiterer had been snuffed out, and replaced by a

lo one overliberated   e evil figur
                                        eeblemindec

stifle my joy of life."   Huysmans," he
come back down."
tisfaction. It unset-   on Decadence,
n. When they were   olist diction, and
emotion, to be sure   assions. She had
influence. Frances   d been treated to
orearmed her. She   d whipping closets
of the bell.   e had stopped Toby
act he usually re-   r of denying literary
?" he asked.   tention of provoking
. "One girl from   on top of the pile of

d. "I'll meet you   od part. He pulled the
                                        ounted them to himself,
nilk. But when   at Frances, his face was
ith misgivings.   im fondly, affirming his
ogether in one   k in puberty, that was all.
se parts of her   the pile. "Forty tomorrow
ck or outrage
not live up to   'd better call him."
ypes and not   aturday night. We can cele-
othold in her
to throw safe   problems. I think he's off for
erself against
oorframe to   s her temporary Boston office,
s she the last   ge manager to call Paul to the
might take
                                        en she had issued the invitation.
                                        at old Pom?"

"I warn you," said Frances, "if you
thing . . ."

"I don't like you," said Paul. "You try to
She was almost in tears. "Just forget it. I'l

Paul heard the break in her voice with sa
tled him when she was away or out of reac
separated, he tried to provoke her to strong
she was still his creature and under no new
knew this pattern, but the knowledge never f
reacted each time like a hamster to the sound

Then Paul let her off the hook, with the t
served for actors. "Did you find any big talent

"I think so." This colleagueship pleased her
Northeastern."

"You read her to me Saturday night," he sai
at the Fosters'."

The rest of the conversation was as easy as r
Frances put down the phone, she was filled w
Did she want Pom and Toby and Paul alone t
room? There was more wisdom in keeping the
life discrete. She was not afraid Paul would sho
other people; she was afraid other people would
Paul. When he was around, she began to see t
individuals. Knowing the Fosters still gave her a fo
own tradition. If they failed her, she would have t
custom aside. Nowadays Frances was measuring he
Paul like a child whose parents cut notches in a d
show him his height from year to year. How tall wa
time she had measured? She wondered how long it
before she would reach him.

. . .

Baby Joshua and little Beth had fallen asleep on the hearthrug, curled together like puppies, with their rumps up. They were still asleep, puffing wetly through their mouths, at eleven o'clock. Dinner had been served very late, though not late according to Pom. She had spent her junior year abroad in Valladolid, which allowed her to declare Spanish hours when she was behind schedule.

Paul had arrived at seven-thirty. Frances kept a wary eye on him while they sat in the living room. He had been raised by a grandmother who believed in demand feeding and a mother who fed him on a rigid program. These rival nurturers had addled his infant metabolism, and anxiety about mealtimes made him prey to a mood he called chemical anger. Frances could see he was in its grip; she knew all the signs. He was jiggling his foot, narrowing his eyes, and taking his pulse. She grew warier and warier, until she had no attention for anyone else. He drank six bottles of diet cola and finished off a basket of humid corn chips. By ten o'clock she feared he might eat the ferns, then start on the children.

At eleven Pom was starting to serve dessert. They were having strawberries, with crème fraîche she had fermented herself. Toby and Paul were leaning back in their chairs and talking. Paul's chemical anger had been appeased by good rare beef. Frances trotted back and forth with dirty plates while Pom chattered, and hulled and halved the berries.

"I asked her if I could make the quiche and she said I've got the quiche, so I said I'd bring the pâté and she told me she had the pâté. Then I told her I'd get the Brie but oh, no, she had the Brie. I don't see what else I could have done, do you, Frances?"

Pom spewed and sputtered like a little teakettle. She was grieving over Mrs. Albion Harwood's self-sufficiency. Pom wanted Toby to be the next president of Harwood. She pushed and worried the issue, and kept it right in the front of her mind. In the same vein, she would tear the cloth when she was cutting out a pattern, lacking the patience to keep opening and closing the scissors. For this reason, mainly, Frances did not believe in the Wards and the De Lessières. Yet why did Pom even hint at them? No true company wife would obstruct her own goal with scandal.

Frances took the bowl of strawberries in both hands, and set her hip against the swinging dining-room door to open it. She stopped at the door sill. Apparently her thoughts had been partially telepathized. Paul was describing the practice of group marriage in the Sinusian Islands. Spite and mischief were upon him, the transmutation of chemical anger. He was going to smoke out the Fosters, those false polygamists.

Briefly, Frances thought of dropping the strawberries. That would halt the conversation, but would it change it? She could hear Toby's drawled responses. She was sure he had on his ape face, the face she hated. So far, Paul was being merely anthropological. It seemed the Sinusians imitated the customs of their ancestor gods. Group marriage, Paul expounded loftily, was of proven benefit to children, who grew up believing all men were truly brothers. These short, gray-skinned islanders had an answer that evaded civilized Westerners. As she stood there eavesdropping, Frances had to stiffen her cheeks to keep from laughing. Delight at Paul's strategy slackened all her governess-reflexes. Clyde Beatty also knew when it was useless to restrain a tiger.

Baby Joshua and little Beth were upstairs in their cribs. To save dishes, Pom brought the coffee in Styrofoam cups. Opposite one another, on facing love seats, sat Toby with Frances, and Paul with Pom. Paul had one arm stretched out behind Pom's back, like a teenager poised to make a snaky move at a drive-in.

Frances dug well into her end of the couch, crossing her arms over her chest and wrapping her legs around each other at the knees and ankles.

Paul still had the floor. He had a look on his face like Suslov, the Soviet military tactician, all mind, burning behind the rimless eyeglasses. Under the force of so much intellectual fervor, Pom slid down in her seat, leaned back, and let the top of her head graze the underside of Paul's arm.

"My community of actors," Paul concluded, "is a group marriage in all but sexual practice. And many of us feel we are almost ready for that ratification."

Toby clamped the back of his hand to his mouth, as if to quell a rush of saliva. "Literary m-movements also have an orgiastic, or pseudo-orgiastic, drive," he said. Frances thought he had told her his early stammer had been cured.

Paul shook his head, and smiled with sweet compassion.

"I'm talking about fellowship, and you bring up degradation."

Frances was dazzled. Paul had mastered the art of shaming intellectuals; all he did was speak the role of the natural man. He had used the same knack with critics: if they disagreed with him, they must be deficient in human feeling. Some of these critics, poor hydrocephalic husks, had appealed to Paul, and begged to be reunited with their bodies. He had undertaken the rehabilitation of several of them, especially the younger ones, who wrote for *Manhattan Showcase*. His biggest success had been Marty Julius, who joined a mime troupe, forswearing the written and spoken word forever.

Frances had never before seen Toby at a loss. He looked like a child in a Christmas pageant whose halo had slipped. He gave her a pleading glance, then addressed himself to Paul.

"You can't involve a girl like Frances in your experiment."

Toby reached for her hand, or as much of her hand as she would extend, the tips of three fingers. He was trying on the cloak of womanhood's knight and champion.

"I've been in on all the planning sessions," said Frances. "I helped draw up the charter. We've even scheduled periods of abstinence, like meatless Fridays." She could see from the flash in Paul's eye that she had passed the audition.

Pom was scratching behind her ears as if she had fleas. Toby had hired a black editor and published Soviet runaways. Many full-page protest ads had appeared in the newspapers, signed by both Fosters. No one had told them about this new movement, or asked them to join. She would have to pipe up, to show that they had the credentials.

"We've been approached," said Pom, as if it were a matter of sorority bidding; "quite recently, too, wasn't it, Toby? Four times, actually, I don't mean by four people, it was two couples twice. We turned them down, didn't we, Toby? We weren't sure they were really committed. Toby said they were dilettantes. Besides, they didn't have any children."

Frances spoke very carefully, because Pom did not trade in logic. "What does childless or not have to do with it?"

"You know, fellowship," said Pom brightly. She was parroting the lesson. "That was the real thing for us, to be a family."

Paul lowered his voice with a crash. "I'll bet you ran like a rabbit." He was turning mean, losing patience with the game just as Frances was learning to play.

"That's the liberal dodge," said Paul, "watching and talking. Mincing around on the edges. All talk and no action."

He got up from his seat so fast he collapsed the cushions. "On your feet, Frances. It's late, I need my sleep."

He nodded and waved, like the Queen from her carriage, as he swept her by the Fosters, the stiff-armed wave with stiff fingers, performed from the elbow. On the stairs Frances wriggled around and looked below. Pom and Toby dangled bleakly in their places, as if their strings had gone slack.

In their room Paul fell on the bed and removed his loafers. He let them drop, one by one, on the floor. They were large, loud shoes.

"You've got no stamina for anything but art," Frances was whining. "All that great material down the drain. You could have held out one more hour."

Paul raised the window and put his head way out. He seemed to be measuring the distance from the sill to the ground.

"They're too easy," he answered, and ducked back inside. "It's like jacking off."

"We can't leave now," said Frances. "We'll go after breakfast."

"I won't sit knee to knee with those owls. Is there a clock in this room?"

"All right, all right." She pointed. "Over there. You set it for six. I can write them a nice bland note."

The moon left a broad white wake across the bed. The shades were up, because Frances could not sleep in the dark. In her own apartment, two and a half rooms and an alcove, she patrolled each night, jerking aside the clothes in the closets, and peering behind the shower curtain. She was not sure if what she feared most was burglars or vampires. She slept deeper with Paul in the bed, but she still needed light. He lay on his side and she pressed up against him, clamping her arm over his chest, fitting her knees into the bend of his legs. They came apart several times in the night, then recombined.

Paul, in sleep, was a nerveless creature. He could have slept through the battle of Midway. He had long refreshing dreams, with plots, in which he shot current enemies with machine guns or set spectacular fires. Sometimes he dreamed a new scene for his play, and would use it intact. Frances believed that coherent dreams were a sign of genius, since her own were vague and disguised, and hung on to make her morbid all day long. No dream-symbol dictionary, popular or learned, had ever helped solve them.

What she saw, at that moment, was a normal image from her dreams. Two pale, bare figures were gliding into the room. Misty, doleful figures, holding hands at the foot of the bed. Frances blinked. The door was open, but she knew Paul had shut it. Her mind was drowsy. Perhaps it was the children, walking in their sleep or wanting a drink of water. Her eyes cleared. She jabbed Paul hard, in the kidneys. He sat up in bed and let out a strangled yelp.

"Hit the deck! They've got guns!"

He was not awake. The two ghostly figures shrank back, but they held their ground. Paul kept one hand on Frances's head, mashing her into the pillow. He thrashed at the sheets with his knees and reached for the bed table.

"Stay down! I've got them!"

He yanked the lamp out of its socket and hurled it. The lamp grazed Toby on one twinkling buttock as the two figures fled.

Paul bounded across the room and threw his body against the door. It slammed with a bang, but no harder than Frances was laughing. She tried to think what Paul could be dreaming. That Indians had surrounded the Conestoga wagon? That the Spanish Inquisition had raided a cell of heretics?

"Wake up!" she called out. "Brave fellow!" Tears of laughter streamed down her face.

"I'm awake," he said. "Get up quick. Those scabby little perverts might come back."

Frances swallowed her laughter. "I thought you were dreaming about Indians!"

"Oh, no," he said, opening the suitcase. "I had to save face. Theirs and ours. I egged them on, after all."

"You're a very great man," said Frances.

"I am if you say so," said Paul. "We make good team-mates."

They packed and dressed in the dark, except for their shoes, and moved out down the hallway barefoot. The house had a flight of back stairs, which did not creak. As they crossed the front lawn toward the car, Paul tripped on the sprinkler. He picked it up by the neck and spoke to it.

"I'm not finished here yet."

He went up the porch steps and set down the sprinkler, aiming it at the door. He screwed it into the fixed position, so it wouldn't revolve. Frances did not have to wait for orders. She followed the hose to the side of the house and opened the spigot.

They watched the shower, for a moment, entranced.

"Can't we lurk across the street and watch them get it?"

Paul yanked her arm for an answer. They got into the car. With the sun coming up, they left Boston, hitting seventy-five miles an hour. It was the first time Frances had ever begged Paul to drive faster.

III
SEX LIFE

F rances was working a night shift and a day shift. By night, she worked for Paul; by day for Harwood. Since Paul was directing *The Winter's Tale* in Kansas, Frances had a month of evenings to herself. The first week, she stayed at home and caught up on her reading. She soaked in the bathtub, since Paul disapproved of baths. She liked steeping with open pores in her own juices. She liked lounging on her bed, with no higher goals or plans. She liked watching Lewis, the black-and-white bob-tailed cat, who could open the kitchen cabinets with his claws. The second week, Frances was busier, but she set her own hours. By the third week, her unscheduled evenings had dwindled to two; the long arm of Paul Treat could reach across half a continent. He needed some books from his library (special delivery), relating to previous productions in Sweden and Moscow. He needed four jars of hand cleanser made with tar, sold only at a druggist's supply house in Bridgeport, Connecticut. He needed a bear for the play (Act III, Scene 3), a live bear, no question of using a man in a bear suit. There was no bear for hire at the Kansas City Zoo. Frances balked at the bear, but she knew *Winter's Tale* by memory; there were shepherds in Act IV, which portended an order for sheep. Frances wondered if the Mortenson Theatre had dismissed its propman, or if Paul set her tasks to test her love and allegiance.

The fourth week was carefree and slothful, like the first week—slothful in Paul's terms, since her work did not benefit him. She rewrote large sections of a manual on healing with gemstones, and stayed up very late indexing a life of the Lunts. Paul's reaching arm and its extension, his dialing finger, were occupied with technical run-throughs and dress rehearsals. At this stage of a play, Frances never had access to Paul. If *The Winter's Tale* were opening in Manhattan, Paul would sleep at the theatre, fully clothed, on the set or in the aisles. If he summoned Frances to his side, he made one condition: no sexual congress until after opening night.

Frances picked up her telephone in the evenings without fear of errands. She started to take her own calls at the Harwood Press. Ruthanne complained. She was bored with typing. She preferred shielding Frances from importunate masculine voices. Paul had sometimes outwitted Ruthanne by disguising his speech, so she had learned to ignore the pleas of any caller with a foreign accent, lisp, or laryngitis. Although Frances's telephone did not need a monitor, her office door was vulnerable and unguarded. Other secretaries' desks sat outside their editors' doors. Ruthanne's desk lay across the room, at a slight diagonal. This position was more effective, as it happened, for keeping watch without overtly spying.

Ruthanne looked up from her typing, alert to danger. She saw the new editor, Allan Schieffman, in Frances's doorway. With his palms against the frame of the door, he pushed in and out, as if to develop the muscles of his arms and chest. He had been there yesterday, and the day before, grasping the top of the doorframe from inside, raising himself off the floor, doing casual chin-ups. Ruthanne Marvin was as loyal as an ocelot. Her loyalty did not stem from blind devotion. She knew, after months of constant observation, that Frances was easy prey to office-hoppers. When Frances listened to people, she looked them in the eye. She did not chew on her pencil or twirl a lock of hair, or glance at the unfinished letter she had been drafting. She was so still, so present, and so attentive that she could have elicited speech from inanimate objects. Ruthanne timed every intrusion by the clock. When ten minutes were up, she called Frances to announce a visitor, or marched into her office with papers that needed her signature. The new editor only stayed for seven minutes, but his gymnastics had aroused Ruthanne's protective instincts. She watched him leave. He toed in when he walked, like an athlete, but his neck was skinny and his shoulders were stooped and narrow.

Ruthanne stood by Frances's desk with her hands on her hips. "He asked you to lunch," she declared. "I could tell from behind."

"He's married," said Frances. "He has two lovely boys, five and seven."

"If he didn't, he will. Pop eyes mean a carnal nature."

"Perhaps he has goiter," said Frances. "Or hypertension."

"I know what he makes," said Ruthanne. "It's a lot more than you do."

"He's older," said Frances. "He brought in all those New Left authors."

"The market is glutted," said Ruthanne, spouting borrowed wisdom.

Frances started to laugh. She pointed at the chair by her desk.

"Sit down, old lady. I give in. You were right, he asked me."

"You can't go," said Ruthanne. "He wears terry-cloth sweatbands on his wrists."

"He won't hurt me," said Frances. "If the restaurant is brightly lit."

"I've heard things," said Ruthanne. Her eyebrows were slanted with anxiety. "I happened to be in the ladies' room, and those hens didn't know I was there. . . ."

"Faster and funnier," said Frances. Ruthanne flopped down in the chair.

"The girl who works for him?"

"Maude Perkins. Or Parsons."

"He made them hire her," said Ruthanne.

"Does this get worse?" said Frances. "Should I close the door?"

"She worked for him at Carver & Duff. He made *them* hire her, too."

Frances stopped teasing Ruthanne. She got down to her level. "His boys are at the French lycée. He said they were 'spookily bilingual.'" Her tone held the quote at arm's length, like a piece of litter.

"I wish that would put you off. But you don't mind affected people."

This odd, piercing remark touched Frances. Ruthanne watched her very closely. In general, close attention made Frances nervous, since the watcher was often looking for faults and finding them. Ruthanne never made black marks or gave gold stars. Ruthanne was twenty and Frances was twenty-seven. From her first day at work, she had made herself Frances's guardian. She believed, like Wordsworth, that wisdom grows less with age; therefore she, not Frances, was rightly the older person. Unlike Paul, Ruthanne cared whether Frances ate lunch with adulterers. The night before he left, Paul had dealt with the subject of fidelity. He stated his views, and Frances had poor luck rebutting them. Since Frances had refused to accompany Paul to Kansas, he believed they should "see other people," or feel free to do so. "I didn't refuse," said Frances. "I can't leave Harwood." "Can't means won't," said Paul. "You're responsible for the subtext." "What does 'see' mean?" asked Frances. "I don't like double binds," said Paul. "Once you make up your mind, you forfeit the right to ask questions."

Frances had an excellent view of her luncheon companion. The restaurant was lit for seeing, like a public library. Allan Schieffman did not look at Frances. He darted glances. He met her gaze, then lowered his eyes before she did. He tilted his head. He stroked the stem of his wineglass. His gestures, in any female, would be called coquettish.

"I can't leave my wife," said Allan, setting down his menu. Frances was so startled that she turned to look around her, in case he had addressed a woman at a nearby table. Allan ducked his chin and spoke to a basket of breadsticks. "I've been watching you," he said. "You have funny looks. On your bad days you're plain, but your good days are very good." He smiled at the breadsticks, a shy, self-mocking smile, as if it were too soon to pay them such a lavish compliment.

Frances froze like a rabbit in the headlights of a speeding car. Her mind went blank, although she noticed Allan Schieffman's teeth. He was thirty-six, but his teeth were in their middle fifties. One canine was chipped and the lower incisors were dark, as if they had fur caps. His mouth was moving, which implied he must be talking. All she could hear was a rushing sound in her ears. Frances was not trained in the art of swift reprisals. She sat there with her teeth in her mouth, and they were sharp, white teeth.

When her hearing came back, Allan Schieffman was telling a story, or the end of a story, in which Norman Mailer had punched him in the stomach, an affectionate punch, and a tribute to his washboard midriff. Allan Schieffman treated Frances to a picture of literary life. Allan's place was in the inner circle, not on the fringes. Saul Bellow had bipped him on the arm to test his biceps. William Styron, who was balding, had tugged at Allan's thick brown hair. No wonder Allan Schieffman practiced chin-ups in her office doorway; he needed to be fit to endure the brutal world of letters.

Allan Schieffman took Frances's arm walking back to Harwood. He cupped her elbow crossing streets when the light turned green. When they reached the building, Allan paused. He was holding keys, a bunch of many keys on a ring with a round brass tag. He weighed the keys on his palm. He tossed them up and caught them. He weighed them, tossed them, and caught them several times in turn.

"They belong to a friend," he said. "He's out of town." He twirled the keys by the tag. They jingled loudly. "We can go there any time," said Allan. "He lives alone."

Up went the keys. Frances grabbed them in midair and caught them. She held them overhead and dropped them from that height onto the sidewalk. They hit Allan's foot, which was shod in a canvas sneaker. Frances turned without a word and pushed through the revolving doors.

Frances Girard had followed Paul Treat's instructions. She had "seen other people," and found them distinctly wanting. She wondered if Paul had issued his instruction in the first place to increase her awareness of his rare and curious nature. Other people were not like Paul. They were vain and random. They lacked Paul's sense of mission and powers of concentration. Frances had never been privileged to know an artist. She had known many writers, but they saw all sides of a question. Paul was never enthralled by doubts or opposing viewpoints. He ran a straight course, keeping close to the inside rail. Now that Frances knew Paul, her own inner discipline had sharpened. In less than a year, she had learned to account for her time. Before Paul, there were hours she had put to no use or purpose. She had had lunch with friends, walked the long way instead of the short way, watched the life of the streets or the patterns of clouds from her window. When she turned out the lights and reviewed the events of the day, she often found there were holes in her memory, gaps of time she had wasted. With Paul in Kansas City, she had backslid on several occasions. Only last Sunday she had eaten her breakfast on a bed tray. She had sat in the park feeding sparrows and sunning her face. Frances burned and peeled in short order. She would have new freckles when Paul got back late Friday night. He would notice her freckles and be sure she had never acquired them in his service or her role as a worker for the Harwood Press.

Several months after Frances met Paul, she began to lose weight. She started losing red blood cells, too, and took doses of iron. She saw Paul every night when she should have been editing or reading. Then she got the idea of mixing romance with homework. One night she appeared at Paul's loft in the brass-fittings building with an armload of manuscripts from Harwood, now long overdue. Paul was writing a play, *Variations on a Primal Scene,* not a play as we know one, but outlines for improvisations. Paul believed that the playwright was passé (except for Shakespeare), and that theatre was a collaboration of director and actors. Paul was seated at his desk ruling lines on a sheet of blank paper. Frances curled up nearby and opened a large box of typescript. After reading several pages, relating to women in communes, she noticed that Paul kept frowning and sending her glances. He was tapping his pencil, too loudly for concentration. When he had broken two pencils, she put her assignment away. Paul looked at Frances, more in sorrow than in anger, and announced that the program for the evening had been disrupted. If she had not preferred to engage in parallel play, they might have advanced the cause of Paul's new project by reading aloud some sections from *Oedipus Rex,* that mother lode of all conjecture on primal scenes. Frances hung her head

and listened while Paul explained that lovers must work together or drift apart. Love was a partnership, based on shared
aims and values. Separate interests were as harmful to love as
infidelity. Paul had never used the word "love" in her connection, which went a long way toward easing her niggling doubts,
such as whether her job at Harwood was a "separate interest,"
along with chores like paying her bills or worming her cat.
Would she get time off? Did Paul ever take a break? Even
tourists on package tours had free days scheduled.

Paul ran a tight courtship, but his standards for himself were
as stringent. When Frances's motor began to cough or idle, she
had his example to shame her back in line. No one had ever
called her a lazy person, though she sometimes took naps after
work for half an hour. She had once gone to sleep at Paul's loft
between work and supper. She awoke in the dark to an uproar
in the kitchen, drawers wrenched open and cutlery rattling, pots
or skillets banged down on the stove, dishes stacked, or un-
stacked, in a way that portended breakage. Over this din she had
heard an evil grumbling, and made out the words "escape" and
"motivation."

In spite of his devotion to work, Paul believed he was lazy—
if not lazy, perhaps hypothyroid, or possibly dead. Since death
might set in by inches, undetected, he had formed the habit of
checking his pulse throughout the day. She had seen him holding his wrist in the soundest sleep, though his chest was rising
and falling at a steady rate. Frances was never sure Paul really
slept, or that his brain, that wakeful giant, became unconscious.
Paul had pointed eyebrows to match his reddish beard. From
the peak of each brow curled a hair, like an antenna, which
twitched during sleep, sending signals to the giant, who decoded
them for Paul into dreams as clear as memos. Asleep or awake,
Paul never seemed dead to Frances, who wished he would take

his lazy tendency to his bosom, embrace it with a fervent heart, and make it his friend. Then she and Paul could go for walks without a camera, taking pictures of odd or demented passersby, whose gestures and grimaces might prove helpful in coaching actors. She and Paul could make conversation in public places, instead of copying overheard gems into spiral notebooks (although Paul had lately lost interest in flavorsome quips and dialect, and had started recording the monotonous quality of functional speech). They could visit museums and galleries for pleasure, stopping to gaze at what was beautiful or new, instead of discussing the composition of every painting, and drawing diagrams that Paul could use for blocking scenes. They could go to a party without a fixed agenda, enjoy meeting new people and exchanging useless small talk, instead of casing the guests according to rank and income, and whether they qualified as backers of modern theatre.

There is one place where lovers are allowed to rest from toil, or so Frances thought until she was undeceived. The bedroom—or, in a loft like Paul's, the bed—should be a refuge, a holiday, and a hiding place. When Frances and Paul first met, they had once spent a day in bed, a whole day of play, athletic and meditative, a white day, the French would say, since sleep was not its object. There had been some white mornings since, and white afternoons, but most of their life in bed was more like work. No matter how warm their embraces at the outset, each session was soon corrupted by goals and tests. One night they were lying in bed, Paul covering Frances. Paul was heavy and tall and Frances was short and thin. He was large enough to crush her, if he had a mind to, but he seemed content to kiss her and stroke her haunches. Frances had begun to stir and press him closer. All at once, Paul rolled over and sat on the edge of the bed. Frances wondered if she had been clumsy—or, worse, unsavory. Perhaps there were patches of chicken skin on her rump.

"I think we should practice cunnilectus," said Paul severely.

Frances started to laugh. She thought Paul must be teasing. "Cunnilectus" (the word) was a recent private joke. Frances had heard it pronounced by a young gynecologist, who felt bound by his oath to give patients some sex-instruction. The same doctor put a u in "spontaneity," where the e ought to be, and told couples they could choose from a "plathora" of sexual positions.

"We did, once," said Frances, "for your play on the incest taboo."

"Wrong for incest," said Paul.

"Is it better for primal scenes?"

"It's for me, not the play. I ought to learn how. They like it."

"If 'they' includes me, you did a good job," said Frances.

"If I practice enough, I might get to like it," said Paul.

"Do you think I'm a sewer? Is that why you hate it?" asked Frances.

"You have to go wash. Perhaps we should shave you," said Paul.

This idea was so striking that Frances forgot her hurt feelings. "In the shape of a heart? In the shape of a bowler hat?"

Cunnilectus (the act) was proving too challenging to Paul. He sought reassurance. He grabbed Frances's wrist and took her pulse as well as his own.

"We could bleach you," said Paul.

"It would sting."

"We could settle for a trim."

This bargaining might have continued until early morning if Paul had not glanced at his copy of *Oedipus Rex*. For the rest of the night, they played Oedipus and Jocasta, stopping short of the blinding of Oedipus and the suicide of the Queen.

. . .

Friday, the day of Paul's homecoming, came too soon. Too soon because Frances had a very long manuscript to edit. The author was a woman doctor with a pitted complexion who thought women had given up control of their menstrual cycles. Dr. Marr disliked Frances, whose skin was unblemished and fair, and argued each point until Frances conceded from weariness. Her arguments were logical, but Frances found their premise wrongheaded. The menses were a natural phenomenon, like the weather, or Paul Treat. She had no more control of her cycles than she did of her weekends. Before Paul, she had met Monday deadlines by working straight through. How would she juggle Paul's claims and her half-finished manuscript? Could she feed him a sedative and work while he slept off its influence? Could she gain a few hours if she invented a visit from Aunt Ada, in town for the day from her house in the Hudson Valley? She remembered, however, that Paul felt, with Jesus Christ, that service to him involved severing family ties. Perhaps she could slip away to the corner grocery, pretending to restock Paul's icebox and his kitchen shelves. She could button a sheaf of manuscript inside her shirt and edit the pages in the dark back booth of a coffee shop. Would Paul rather be betrayed for a manuscript or a man? On the whole, Frances thought he would not admit the difference.

Late Friday night, Frances climbed the five flights to Paul's loft. Carrying a suitcase and a bottle of wine, she scratched at his door; it was made of solid steel, with no bell or knocker. If Paul did not answer in a minute, she would kick or pound. The door flew open. A tall figure loomed in the half-light.

"Brutal beast!" cried Paul, and wrapped her in his mighty arms.

"Large and fair," said Frances, hugging him with wine and suitcase. She rubbed her face against his coat until her left cheek burned. Paul gnawed the top of her head and chafed her ears.

"I forget how blonde," he said as he patted her hair.

For an hour they kissed and grappled on Paul's sofa. They drank the wine. Paul read her his reviews. Paul's *Winter's Tale* had frightened Kansas City—not the bear (trained and live), but the shepherds' groins, which were bearded. Paul had pasted false hair on their legs and lower torsos, and studded the tufts with berries, weeds, and field flowers. Frances beamed with pride. She butted her head against his shoulder. Here they were, conversing, even chatting, like a normal couple, bending Time to their will, taking flagrant liberties with Time. After only an hour of friendly ease and leisure, she began to imagine a day, a week, a month. Her vision was interrupted by a steady creaking. Paul was jiggling his foot and making the couch springs vibrate. He slapped his palms on his knees and prepared to rise.

"Well," said Paul. "Are you ready to do the arson?"

"Right now?" asked Frances.

"While it's fresh in my mind," said Paul. He dug in his pockets and fished out bits of paper, halves of envelopes, backs of matchbooks, and shredded napkins. He sorted through them and laid some on the table, arranging the scraps like the pieces of a picture puzzle. While directing a play, Paul always worked on the next one, scrawling new ideas on any handy surface. While *The Winter's Tale* was being rehearsed and mounted, *Variations on a Primal Scene* was taking form.

Frances had no experience of primal scenes, though Paul insisted that she was blocking out the memory. Her parents had slept in single beds with monogrammed spreads, and opened their door at night for ventilation. Paul's mother and father shared a double bed, the covers of which were always mussed or pushed aside ("enseamèd bed," said Paul, reciting *Hamlet*). At night their door was closed, and little Paul, who should have been tucked in and dreaming sweetly, was drawn from his own warm bed toward the taboo portal, rooted at the threshold by the sounds of lewdness, quick gasps, sharp sighs, grunts, moans, and bouncing bedsprings. With both small fists he tried to turn the doorknob, and found the door was bolted from inside. His eyes were almost level with the keyhole, but the room was dark, or the hole had been plugged up. One night, after many vigils, Paul boiled over. He took what he called the "only-child's revenge." (It was his theory that children with siblings had other outlets, and were far less likely to witness primal scenes.) Little Paul set a box of matches on the doorsill. He opened the box and struck a match. He dropped it in. He watched the matches hissing into flame; then he ran on his tiptoes back to his nursery room. The house had not burned, and Paul was alive to tell the tale. After that night, Paul often slept in his parents' bed, a state of affairs that made him a director, since directors were all voyeurs, according to textbooks.

From the fragments contained in the pockets of his jacket, Paul had outlined the core event of his primal play. In order to explore this psychic raw material, he set the stage with Frances as his stagehand. The couch was the marriage bed; a chair Paul's cot. A bookcase would represent the Door of Doors. Paul acted out the spying and the arson, and Frances took notes because he might remember something new, such as jabbing his finger into the darkling keyhole, and kneeling to peer through the space between doorsill and door. At one point Paul introduced an innovation. He pretended to pee on the matches to put them out. He declared himself pleased with this tricky piece of business, which would play if the actor in question was turned upstage. Many boxes of matches were consumed during these experi-

ments. They left a blackened area on the floor. Later on, Paul
asked Frances to do the bedroom noises. At first, she did them so
lamely that Paul started yelling, like the skipper of a sailboat
who is stuck with a novice crew. Little by little, she produced
better sexual music. She could gasp staccato and grunt up and
down the scale. Paul applauded when she made an especially
low-pitched moan, and made her repeat it until she lost her
voice.

On Monday, Frances was hoarse but Dr. Marr was finished,
except for its index and its twelve-page list of women's clinics.
Paul had granted Frances a reprieve on Sunday afternoon, and
left the loft to haggle with a theatre-owner. At the office, Frances noticed that all the desks were empty, as if the secretaries had
gone out on strike. She put her purse and Dr. Marr on
Ruthanne's chair, and set off down the hall to get a cup of coffee.
She passed by Mr. Harwood's office. He was pacing, which
meant that he was hating authors or their agents. Hammy
Griner was eating doughnuts. Allan Schieffman's office door
was closed, but he was out of town. When she had passed his
door, she heard a hiss. She turned. The door had opened several
inches. A skinny arm reached out and crooked a skinny finger.
Frances followed where it led and slithered through the opening.

The arm belonged to Mary Land, who worked for Hammy
Griner. Mr. Harwood's secretary, Delma Dunbar, was rum-
maging in the center drawer of Allan's desk. She found an envelope, or airmail letter, and gave it to Ruthanne, who held three
others. Mary Land, who had forgotten her reading glasses, was
bending over a sheet of stationery, colored pink. Delma brought
out two picture postcards and waved them high. Ruthanne
snatched one and went to the window to read it better. Frances
cleared her throat to capture their attention.

"I want to thank you all for electing me ship's doctor."

Three pairs of eyes looked up, then went on reading.

"It's not an elective position," Delma said.

"Listen to this," said Mary; "so disgusting. 'I feel you deep inside me on the subway.'"

"Shoof," said Delma. "Try this on for size. 'I've counted ten thousand minutes since you left me.'"

"Where's Maude?" asked Frances, referring to Allan's help-meet.

"Out sick," said Mary. "That subway one's from her."

Ruthanne gave Delma a letter postmarked India. "Read Frances the part about 'your skin on mine.'"

"What a haul," said Frances. "How did you get so lucky?"

"Hammy wanted the Vietnam file," said Mary Land.

"Oh, ho," said Frances, "and your eye just happened to fall . . ."

"It did!" Mary twisted her bracelet. "Yours would, too."

Delma got up and collected the cards and letters. She scanned them for content and dealt them into separate piles. She pointed at each pile and named it, starting left to right.

"Two suicide threats, three breakdowns, two abortions. One broken marriage and one bad auto accident."

"No actual deaths," said Ruthanne. "He must be slipping."

"Make copies," said Frances, "and mail them to his house."

"Men," said Mary.

"White boys," gloated Delma.

"Stick it in your ear," said Mary. "They're all the same."

That night Frances hurried to Paul feeling smug and guilty. She was favored above most women, though undeserving. Other men were to Paul as red glass to a ruby. Ordinary men were blurred in spirit and contour. They were not defined, like Paul, by a true vocation. Their energies were scattered, or turned to scurvy uses. Time hung heavy on their hands, so adultery was their hobby. Every impulse or notion had the weight of their fondest ambition, whereas Paul's idlest whims served as fodder for his chosen work. Sometimes Frances was fodder, too, though more often a stable-hand. Paul's work was a glutton with a faultless digestive system. It could process rich foods, like adultery, into scenes or stage values. Leaner portions, like nightmares or fantasies, could be used direct. In a sense, Frances had two masters, Paul and Paul's art. Other women might never know that satisfaction. She did not have to fear Paul's habit of stealing dinner knives, or his interest in the demographics of prostitution. She was not concerned by his horror of having his thumbs held. When he tried to raise funds from strangers, she rested easy. Any flaw in the man would be mended in the work of art.

Frances let herself into Paul's loft with renewed dedication. The object of her dedication stood beside the bed. He was deep in thought, so she did not run to embrace him. There was a halo of light around his head, perhaps from the lamp. Frances marveled, as she often had, at his force of mind. Paul solved problems by thinking. He could think for hours on end, uninterrupted. Frances herself could not think without moving her lips. She thought out loud, addressing herself as "darling." Other mortals thought in fits and starts. Their thoughts bobbed like corks, then capsized under waves of distraction. Frances pictured Allan Schieffman's mind attempting thought. His ideas would founder quickly, swamped by images from his libido: a flash of thigh, a tear-stained cheek, a razor blade, a thin white ankle.

Frances waited like a sentry at the citadel of Paul's reflections. What concept engaged him? Would it change the course of theatre history? Paul was turned away. She crept a little closer to him. He was pondering a pair of shoes that were sitting upright on a table. They were women's shoes, black leather pumps, with pointed toes and sharp high heels. Paul placed his hands inside the shoes and made them walk across the table. He made them do a mincing walk. He made them do a slow half-turn. He made them do a two-step, sideways, and what looked to Frances like a dip. This was curious behavior, surely, but artists were inspired by trifles. She had seen Paul take a pocket mirror and conceive a set for Shakespeare's *Tempest*.

Paul acknowledged Frances. "Put these on."

"Are they part of a primal scene?" asked Frances.

"Maybe. Maybe not," Paul said. "They tilt the female pelvis forward."

Frances forced her feet inside the shoes. Her feet were hot. The pumps were narrow. She grabbed Paul's arm to keep her balance.

"Suppose I trip and fall?" asked Frances.

Paul walked away. He picked up a wooden chair. He counted off twenty paces and then sat down. He made a slit in front of his eyes with his thumb and forefinger, as if he were looking through a viewfinder, or a lens.

"Turn around," said Paul.

Frances shuffled slowly in a circle.

"No good," said Paul. "The clothes are wrong. The clothes come off."

Frances bent her right leg, like a stork. Her right shoe pinched. She bent her left leg. The left shoe was rubbing her heel. Was this work? Or an exercise destined to end in bed? She wished Paul liked his pleasure, as she did, plain vanilla. She felt naked enough already. She did not want to strip. What could she strip? She was not wearing elbow-length gloves. There was no kit of feathers in the loft, stashed away for emergencies. She had only two layers to peel, or a layer and a half, since she never wore slips or brassières and refused to wear stockings.

"What's your problem?" barked Paul. "Take them off! Strut your stuff! Hump the door!"

Paul's loft had no closet. His clothes hung on racks rolled on casters. The entrance and exit to the loft was the heavy fire door, which would slam shut and crush her before she was in position. Paul was asking too much, but he asked even more from his actors. A good actress would find a solution; she would not be so literal. In the absence of doors, a real actress would hump empty air.

"Bump and grind!" shouted Paul. "Just don't die on me!"

"Leave me alone," said Frances. "I don't know how."

Paul wiped a weary palm across his forehead. His lofty brow was creased with lines of woe. He gazed at Frances, or, rather, at the wall behind her. His eyes had faded to a paler shade of blue. If Frances had walked on the ceiling or practiced birdcalls, she would not have regained one atom of his attention. Paul had plans for the shoes. His scheme had failed, thanks to Frances. He saw her, at the moment, as a snag or a hitch in his plans, like a leading man's cold, or a loose wire somewhere in the light-board. Paul was never deterred by failure on a small or large scale. When one project bogged down, he set right to work on another. Leaving Frances to hobble to a chair and remove the shoes, he unfolded a list and began dialing telephone numbers. Until he could balance a failure with a stroke of luck, he was as lost to Frances as if he were still in Kansas. There was nothing for her to do but go home and wait. Before she went out, she performed a stealthy action. She took the black shoes and stuffed them deep in the garbage, in case Paul tried calling an actress who would come and wear them, and reveal their potential for tilting her pelvis forward.

. . .

On Saturday morning, Frances curled up on her window seat. She never looked long before seeing some distracting incident, a pair of transvestites, or a nice arrest, if she was lucky. Across the street, at the Hellman Planetarium, a figure—male?—was leaning out the window. He was lowering a bundle attached to a length of rope. There was no one waiting below to catch the bundle. Frances watched as the package bumped its way down the wall. It disappeared out of sight behind a shrub. She waited for a furtive hand to seize the package. Perhaps she had uncovered a traffic in lunar ores. The man in the window had gone, though the rope still dangled. Perhaps it was only a method of trash disposal. She waited for a sign, but the plot did not develop. Paul would never have allowed the plot to dangle loose. Paul would call the planetarium to report it. He would call the police in a free-form Balkan accent. Holding a pair of binoculars to improve his vision, he would sit and wait for the plotlines to converge.

Without Paul, Frances felt like a story with pages missing. She depended on Paul to make life cohere, like art. Right now Lewis, her cat, was providing entertainment. He was nudging the books off the lower bookcase shelf. *Dracula* toppled over, then Conrad's *Victory,* followed by a copy of *Little Women* with a broken spine. Lewis began to work on a heavier volume, Berenson's *Italian Painters of the Renaissance.* In a moment, the book fell open on the floor. Lewis bolted before he was flattened underneath it. Male animals grappled with life, as did Lewis and Paul. Frances, the female, looked on, or picked up what they dropped. As she knelt on the rug fitting books in their proper slots, she felt dull and light-headed, resourceless in body and spirit. Her body and mind mirrored woman's historic passivity:

the fatigue, the dejection, the limpness, the indecision. She sat with a book on her lap and turned over the pages. She set the book down. She opened another. She closed it. Her muscles were aching from the effort of holding a book. Her forehead was hot but her shoulders were rippling with chills. She thought she might faint. Her throat was too sore to swallow. Was her sore throat a manifestation of a slavish nature? Was she suffering from lack of a penis, or a new strain of flu? It was cheering to think that her ills were somatic, not psychic. She could go to bed guiltless, instead of attempting autonomy.

Wearing socks, a wool bathrobe, a ski cap, and angora mittens, Frances lay under three heavy blankets and a small Turkish rug. At one point she eyed a large portrait (her great-aunt, in jodhpurs), and wondered if paint-coated canvas might supply extra warmth. She tried to lure Lewis to climb up and press in beside her; he had eaten his dinner and his body was laden with calories. Lewis offered no comfort. He snapped at her beckoning mitten. He pounced on her feet when they twitched underneath the thick covers. As always when Frances was sick and unable to eat, she felt a pure craving for lobster and mayonnaise salad.

"They won't let me be sick," Frances moaned as the telephone rang. It was Edie, her friend and her scourge, who now called her twice weekly. Edie's calls were invariably ill-timed, or perhaps they were timed to perfection, since they always caught Frances off guard and more liable to influence.

"They Made Him A Judge," opened Edie, in Biblical tones.

"Who a what?" answered Frances.

"I thought you'd be pleased," chided Edie.

"Hit me again," Frances said.

"Hill. My husband," said Edie. "A federal judge. At his age. He's the youngest in history."

"I am pleased," Frances said. "Please congratulate Hill. What an honor."

"You're depressed," Edie stated, alert to the scent of affliction.

"I'm sick. I'm in bed."

"I'll drop by on my way to the market."

"There's no need, Edie, really."

"Don't try to play possum," said Edie. "I hear how you sound. It's your friend. He's not good for you, Frances."

"What's a nice girl like me . . ." Frances left the trite question unfinished.

"We don't visit," said Edie. "You used to come sit in my kitchen."

"I don't want to wrangle," said Frances. "I have a high fever."

"I'll stop," Edie said, "if you'll give me a sensible reason."

"Don't expect sense," Frances said, "from a germ-ridden person. I want to be shot from a cannon. I want to be aimed like an arrow."

"That's very exalted," said Edie. "Have you taken some aspirin?"

"Be quiet," said Frances, who was seeing her life in a vision. "Paul is the arrow and the bow. He's the archer. He's the bull's-eye. What am I? I'm not even the feathers. Or the straw in the target."

Later on, Frances couldn't remember this brief conversation, or Edie's concern that the fever had scrambled her brain cells. After Edie hung up, Frances fell fast asleep within seconds. She slept on and off for a night and a day, by her reckoning. She saw sights that her well self was blind to, like bugs on the ceiling. These same bugs hung in swags from the bedposts or swarmed on the carpet. The reading chair changed its position, inching forward or backward. When her fever had lowered, Frances sat up and looked in a mirror. She had lost all her color, and her pale hair lay as flat as an otter's. Sitting up was too hard, so she gave in and went back to sleep. Very soon she was dreaming strange dreams of escaping from captors. From the waist up, the captors were bears; from the waist down fork-leggèd. Dreams of flight and pursuit changed to dreams of explosions and warfare. A battering ram was pounding a fortress to rubble. The cat entered the dream. He streaked through the doorway in terror. He jumped on her pillow—her real pillow, not its dream image. Her physical ears heard a thud at her tangible front door. Whoever was kicking the door was leaning on the doorbell. They could take what they liked if only they stopped making that noise.

The front door gave way with a bang. It slammed shut just as loudly. The vandal swore ditto: "Goddamnit, you gave me bum keys!" Paul's footfall was weighty. The carpet resounded like marble. He barged into her room, then drew back, taking shelter in the doorway.

"What's this?" Paul looked frightened. "What's the story?"

"I have fever and chills," answered Frances.

"Where's the vitamin C?" asked Paul. He pulled out a handkerchief.

"It's gone," Frances said. "Please don't go."

Paul covered his nose. "You look pretty when you're weak," he said. "Perhaps I should prey upon you."

"I ache," begged Frances.

"Bliss might unkink you," said Paul. He sat on the edge of the bed and felt for her breasts.

"I'm cold." Frances squirmed away. "I have chills and fever."

Paul pulled back his hand. He looked at it closely and shook it, for fear it was crawling with leggy black septic microbes.

"I better go wash," said Paul. "Are your towels infected?"

"Use the bathmat," said Frances.

"With feet on it?"

"Use the tissues."

"They shred," said Paul. He turned on the hot and cold faucets.

Frances called out, "You're wasting a lot of water."

"I don't trust the soap." Paul was wiping his hands on his trousers.

Paul picked up a straight-backed chair. He parked it beside the bed. He sat down and looked at Frances with a mixture of pity and appraisal.

"Poor brute," he said. "How sick are you?"

"A hundred and two," said Frances.

"Too sick to play Rudolf and Mary?"

"Much too sick," said Frances. "Who are they?"

"I got a water pistol, just in case. You can't buy a gun on Sunday."

Frances tried to remember. Rudolf. Rudolf and Mary. Mary?

"Do you have any candles?" asked Paul. "To do it right, we need fifty."

"I'm not on props," muttered Frances. She began to remember, dimly.

"He shot her in the temple," said Paul. "He shot himself three hours later."

Frances slid far beneath the covers. Only her eyes were showing. In her mind's eye she pictured Mayerling, and the agony of Rudolf of Hapsburg. His mistress, the Baroness Mary, dressed for bed in ribbons and laces. Writers loved Rudolf and Mary, and their nasty romantic suicide. Many books probed the mystery of Mayerling. Did the Prince lose his nerve, like Hamlet? Did he fire two shots, or just one? Did assassins lurk in the azaleas? Frances wished for a bed in a hospital, guarded by nurses, where suicide games, like rich foods, were forbidden to patients.

Paul was pacing the room in frustration. When inspired, he

was apt to be testy. He viewed Frances's virus as a hindrance; was she out of commission, or obstructive? Frances knew that he saw her as no better than a backer who has welshed on his investment. Paul prowled through the living room and kitchen, pulling out drawers but not closing them. He returned and went back to the bathroom. She could hear him ransacking the cabinet. He emerged with a vial of brown liquid. He leaned over Frances and opened it.

"Iodine," said Paul. "For the wound."

Frances flinched as he dabbed at her temple. She was glad Paul had settled for iodine, which would come off with soap and hard scrubbing. He had not found the can of red paint, which was sticky, like blood, and dried slowly.

"Could we do this tomorrow?" asked Frances. "I can't act when I'm sick. I can't help you."

"You're playing a corpse." Paul kept dabbing. "You don't have to act. You just lie there."

"I don't understand," pleaded Frances. "How do primal scenes fit in with suicide?"

Paul peered at the wound he had painted. He was satisfied with its dimensions. "Can't I have two ideas at a time? I need to investigate the love death."

Frances groaned. Paul was not a good doctor. Death and suicide were not healing notions. She wished for an ordinary lover, who made tea and administered back rubs. When Paul appeared, she had been convalescent. She had believed there was hope for recovery. After less than an hour in his care, her germs had regained their vitality.

"What's the love death?" asked Frances. "Is it catching?"

"It's German," said Paul, looking scornful.

"Like the measles," she nodded. "I never had them."

"Can't you muster a little detachment?"

"My resistance is low," whimpered Frances.

"It's not a disease. It's a feeling."

"Adults get them worse," said Frances.

Paul was reaching the end of his patience. If Frances were an actress, he would fire her.

"Get out of your body," ordered Paul. "It's when dying is the same as coming."

"Not in my case." Frances felt her forehead.

"Or when coming is the same as dying."

Frances glanced at him with fresh suspicion. Her sickbed was a rack of nails. Paul had not disclosed his full agenda. He was planning a new set of trials.

"I'm dead already," Frances reasoned. "I'm Mary. Mary's dead. She's dead to sex."

Paul pulled down the blinds on the windows. He turned off every lamp except one. He sat on the edge of the mattress, pitching Frances abruptly to one side. He settled her flat on her back; then he cocked his finger and thumb. He pointed his finger like a pistol and aimed at the iodine wound. He made popping sounds, mimicking bullets. In the process, he jabbed Frances's head.

"That's the end." Frances pushed off his hand. Paul aimed at his own head and fired.

"Alone with the corpse of his lover." Paul was locked in the grip of a theory. "What was he doing for three hours? Passing the time reading Goethe?"

"I'm highly contagious," said Frances.

"He died in the saddle," said Paul.

"You'll get germs if you try it," said Frances. "I'm infectious and so is my area."

This appeal to Paul's health went unheeded. Any artist took risks for his art. Michelangelo was frightened of heights, yet

he spent four long years on a scaffold. Paul bent over her.
Frances recoiled. His eyes were aflame like a martyr's. How
much easier, urged her weak body, to submit to Paul's noble
experiment. She had always been pliant and obliging. She
had worked with good will for Paul's interests. She worked
overtime, double time, and weekends. She worked without
benefits or pensions. In a just world, he owed her a sick leave.
He owed her two weeks with full pay. She deserved a certificate
or a pin, such as volunteers get for long service.

Paul was gifted with powers of telepathy. "I'll give you a
present. Or lamb money."

"Lamb money?" Frances repeated.

"For being a lamb," wheedled Paul.

Frances ducked as Paul reached for her shoulder. Quick as a
snake, she escaped him. She ran into the bathroom and locked it.
Just in time. Paul had vaulted the bed.

"I'll do something to Lewis!" yelled Paul.

"No, you won't!" shouted Frances. "I know you."

He banged on the door with his fists. Frances caught the
words "lose" and "abandon." He rattled and tugged at the doorknob. Frances heard a low animal whimper.

"Come out and I'll soothe you," begged Paul. "I'm a bully.
You hate me."

"No more!" Frances cried. "Not tonight. I hate Rudolf and
Mary."

Frances collapsed on the bathmat. She was out of retorts and
of stamina. She sank back in the grasp of the virus (on the whole,
a more comforting lover). Behind the door, Paul had subsided.
She expected a stronger assault. Had he located the screwdriver
in her toolbox? Would he lift the door off its hinges? Instead,
Frances heard a soft scratching. She looked down at the source
of the noise. Paul was forcing a square piece of paper inch by

inch through the slit at the doorsill. The paper was blank. She reversed it. It was a snapshot: herself at the zoo. The paper was wrinkled and battered. Did Paul keep her picture in his wallet? If Paul kept her picture, he loved her. She loved Paul, though the term was fallacious. She was staggered by Paul, or pervaded. The term "love" was for mothers and children. Why had Paul shown her the snapshot? It meant he forgave her defection. She looked at her image in the picture: a happy girl, eager and toothy. The toothy girl lacked command presence. She said no; the world heard it as maybe.

Frances pondered too long. She was weary. Her instincts were blunted and stupid. She heard footsteps retreating. A door slammed. Her front door, or a nearby apartment's. Paul had left, or pretended to leave. If she came out of hiding, he might trap her. Perhaps he had gone for a locksmith. More likely, he had fixed his sights elsewhere; suicide, double or single, was just one of the sources of high drama. Frances had foiled his attempt to study Suicide; that left thirty-five more Dramatic Situations. Which would Paul choose? Revenge? Revolt? Abduction? Hatred of Kinsmen, False Suspicion, or Fatal Imprudence? She might like to explore Abduction when she was better. She hoped against hope Paul would do Revenge without her.

Frances Girard spent the night locked in the bathroom. She slept in the tub, which she lined with layers of towels. She covered herself with the plastic shower curtain, and folded the bathmat underneath her head. In her porcelain bed, which felt as soft as goosedown, she slept through the night and most of the following morning, like a child who has watched the snow outside his window and knows there will be no school till the storm is over.

IV

LOVE LIFE

Frances was sharing Paul's loft in the old warehouse building, at a ratio of six to one, one part to Frances. Frances's share was divided into smaller sections: a drawer in the bureau; half a shelf in the bookcase; the space beneath the bed and armchairs; a slot in the toothbrush holder; and a steamer trunk for storing spare blankets. When she moved in with Paul, she sent Lewis to board with Aunt Ada. Paul was frightened of fleas, which were hard to distinguish from soot, and more frightened that Lewis would suck his breath while he slept. Since Paul kept bees in a hive on the fire-escape landing, Frances retained some access to non-human creatures. When the skies were clear, the bees were mild and harmless; on overcast days they raged and stung their keeper. Paul took pride in working the hive without veil or gloves, and bore their stings with stoic calm and patience. These days, Paul was spending the bulk of his time with the bees. He tinkered with the hive like a watchmaker in retirement, making needless improvements and averting imaginary problems. He liked to requeen the hive to increase its yield, and ordered new queens from mail-order houses in Georgia. He fed the bees antibiotics in sugar water, to keep them from sickening with dysentery or foulbrood. He added a swarm of Italian bees to the hive, since Italians resisted disease better than Caucasians. In the name of perfection, Paul worked the bees very hard, as hard as he drove the actors he directed. Directors and beekeepers have characteristics in common, as do actors and bees, who submit to the roles assigned them. Each beehive and each production is a little kingdom, and Paul was accustomed to ruling them absolutely.

Without kingdoms to rule, a monarch grows wan and fretful. Governing bees, however disease-resistant, was no substitute for directing human actors. Paul overworked the hive as compensation. One day the bees struck back and took their vengeance. Frances was reading. She heard a strangled whinny, like a horse who is trapped in his stall when fire breaks out. She looked up and saw Paul leaping through the window with a scarf or snood of bees swarming around his head. He crossed the floor in a series of *grands jetés,* very graceful for a heavy man in his predicament. He stood in the shower, howling and lamenting, until he had gained relief for his face and scalp. Little bee bodies clung to his beard and lined the bathtub. Paul was weeping because he had been obliged to drown them.

The theatre had turned on Paul like the angry bees. Bald men in suits claimed his plays went over budget. Producers resented Paul's lack of hospitality. He had ejected more than one backer from rehearsals. Paul treated the moneymen with plain contempt. Producers, like teenagers, liked to voice opinions. In Paul's view, a backer had enough reward by serving the new ideas of men of vision. If Frances urged tact, or at least polite indifference, Paul responded by plotting public scorn and outrage. One of them, Daniel Matthei, a rich man's son, had presumed he and Paul were intellectual equals. He made suggestions—or, worse, offered solutions, and handed Paul pages of script he had rewritten. After several such incidents Paul had wadded the pages, had spat on them lightly, and polished his shoes, tops and soles.

When Paul bit the hand that backed him, Frances trembled.

Frances was a sheep, though her sheep's clothing often bound her. At the sight of Paul's towering pride and indignation, her own heart swelled and applauded his intemperance. In an artist, a haughty streak was a mark of caste. Paul's gifts gave him rights; Frances borrowed acclaim from others, from the authors who wrote the books she was hired to sponsor. She sponsored Paul for love instead of wages. Her wages, in fact, kept Paul as well as Frances. Paul was not too proud to live on Frances's earnings. "I'm a cripple," said Paul. "I only have one skill. Do you want me to drive a taxi or wait on tables?"

Where his art was concerned, Paul was humble and subservient. He worked long hours, though his hope of reward was fading. Lesser artists lapsed into sloth when their hopes were blighted; they ate from tin cans and neglected their personal grooming. They drew spirals and Chinese boxes, and wasted paper; they sighed heavy sighs, in case the world was listening. Paul trimmed his beard and pared his nails and toenails. While he took his shower, he also steamed his trousers. He rose at seven and tended the bees after breakfast; then he spent several hours reading memoirs and lives of great men. After lunch, a monkish meal of cheese and apples, he sat at his desk and took notes for his suicide play. On good days he outlined whole scenes with their final blocking; on bad days he rewrote the notes and revised the revisions. Frances watched him with tears in her eyes. They were tears of awe. An artist who was out of favor should have sour breath, or bloodshot eyes, or dirt on the back of his neck. By rights, he should pore through boxes of yellowed clippings, or gaze in a trance at his wall of framed awards. Paul never complained or reviled his fellow directors. He did not fall asleep in his chair. He drank plain water.

Day after day, Paul mulled over cases of suicide, single and double, successful and unsuccessful; suicide in children and animals (lemmings and whales); suicide by knife, gun, gas, fire, rope, or adder. Frances checked him for signs of despair induced by his subject, such as playing with scissors, or stockpiling bottles of aspirin. Always before, Paul chose themes of a sexual nature: the incest taboo; primal scenes; or the spoiling of virgins. Sex (plus aggression), as a topic, was happier than suicide, since sexual exploits contained an impulse toward life. Frances was anxious, although she curbed her worries. She took off her shoes in the loft and walked on tiptoe. She wrapped the clock in a towel to dull its ticking. She tried not to rustle the pages while she was reading. When she read, she kept one eye on Paul, like a nurse on night duty. Paul paid no attention to Frances unless she addressed him.

In better times, Paul had had numerous uses for Frances. He requested her favors at night or upon awakening. He solicited Frances on many occasions and surfaces. He craved her indulgence in plain and in fancy positions. He possessed an inquiring spirit in carnal matters that nourished his powers of invention in staging theatre. Once, he had tattooed Frances with felt-tipped markers to see if the effect was exciting or repellent. Sometimes he borrowed a motion-picture camera, set it on a tripod, and left it aimed and running. He found that performing for a viewer, albeit mechanical, in no way curtailed the range of his sensations. Frances liked mating in private and in the darkness, without benefit of cameras, mirrors, false hair, or vegetables, but she would have dialed Ronnie's Costume Rentals with her own finger, rather than live with Paul as brother and sister.

In normal times Frances had assisted Paul in his work, by enacting parts from his plays, or bits of staging. Several months had gone by since Paul had allowed her to help, even when she had offered her services as Sylvia Plath. Now and then, Paul would speak of his project if Frances urged him. He had hatched an original theory about Abraham Lincoln. By piecing together stray data contained in footnotes, Paul decided that Lincoln had hired John Booth to shoot him. Frances listened and nodded, as she did when Paul related the tale of the suicide pact of his aunt and uncle, who loved Nature and had chosen her as their executioner. In the summer of their eightieth year, a season of storms, they had walked across treeless fields to attract the lightning, standing wrapped in tight embrace as a squall grew nearer, so that one bolt would claim them both and leave no survivor. Paul's eyes never left her face as he told the tale. When he finished the story, his silence seemed expectant. Frances feared he might ask her to sign a similar pact, and lure her outside when the skies were dark and cloudy. If given the choice, she would rather play Anna Karenina, an exercise that could be carried out indoors with the aid of a ladder laid flat on the floor, for the train tracks, and a teakettle whistling, as the noise of the onrushing train.

Soon Frances and Paul would be living like mice in a garret. Paul had no savings, and editors made meager salaries. A large man required good red meat to succeed in the theatre. For weeks she had stoked his ambitions with beans and potatoes. Frances did laundry in the bathtub, including the sheets. Since washing the sheets bore a strenuous resemblance to wrestling, she took off her clothes and climbed in the tub along with them. As the mistress of an artist, she lacked certain valuable skills. She could not turn frayed cuffs, cobble shoes, or change typewriter ribbons. The right helpmate for Paul would have shoplifted with a clear conscience, or bought day-old bread and made one tea bag stretch for three cups. Frances bought day-old flowers, in the hope they might gladden Paul's spirits, but the flowers made Paul sneeze, since most artists are subject to allergies. Frances hid unpaid bills in a drawer. Paul preferred to outwit their creditors. He might mail off the checks in good time, but leave out the sum or his signature. Or he stacked all the checks in one pile and the envelopes in another. Then he shuffled the piles, so the doctor got a check for the bookstore, or the landlord received partial payment for filling a tooth.

Whether daring or crafty, these tactics eroded Paul's patience—not the tactics so much as the straits that required their contrivance. One night Frances sat reading a manuscript sent by a poet. In order to analyze the rhythms, she spoke some lines under her breath. "You are muttering against me," said Paul as he loomed up behind her. He stalked out of the loft, overturning a lamp as he went. Paul grew restive and wild-eyed. He paced up and down in the loft. He paced on the fire-escape landing, which measured eight steps forth and back. He stooped as he walked, or grimaced and limped like a gargoyle, shutting one eye and jutting his lower teeth forward. He took on the shape of the goblin that lived within him, a vexed, crooked imp, disparaged and disappointed. Paul coined a name for the demon that gnawed at his innards. The imp's name was Nip: Nip Fausto the Overreacher. Living with Nip kept Frances alert and off balance. Nip was not as responsible as Paul, since Nip had no conscience. Frances might rise in the morning and find the loft empty. Her eyes fogged with sleep, she might open the door to the bathroom. Some days she might pad to the sink to perform her ablutions, but one of those mornings she would freeze on the threshold in horror. Nip (and Paul) would be lying in a tub filled with bloody red water, head lolling, mouth open, complexion as pallid as mushrooms. Nip had worked this illusion with packets of raspberry jello. Nip chortled as Frances screamed, but Paul begged her pardon. "He gets out," pleaded Paul. "I can't help it. He makes me obey him." Nip sometimes tossed eggs out the window, or cold mashed potatoes. Nip enjoyed setting broomstraws on fire, and wearing his trousers on backward. Nip rolled himself up in a rug, and lay waiting for Frances to find him. Paul might pull Frances to him and kiss her; as they kissed, Nip would pass her a grape. Frances lived in some dread of Paul's kisses. What if Nip chose to pass her chewed honeycomb?

Nip had two faces, like the masks that are emblems of Drama. One was roguish, or comic, and one was pathetic, or tragic. Tragic Nip—the small child within Paul—believed Frances might leave him, that she might not return from the office, or the shop on the corner. Every evening at six he positioned himself on the sidewalk, one eye on his wristwatch and one on the exit to the subway. If she carried an oversized handbag to work in the morning, he checked it for a toothbrush, a nightgown, and a change of clean clothing. Frances tried to be patient, since Paul and sad Nip were in crisis. She tried to get home right on time, or, if possible, earlier. One night when the subway broke down, she arrived an hour late. Nip was crouched on the steps of the building, weeping in sorrow. "I've abused your good nature!" he cried, "I've exceeded your limits." His apologies worried her more than his devilish hoaxes.

Nip retreated, in time, to the cavernous depths of Paul's psyche. He was shortly replaced by the Tod Hassen (which Paul told her was German for Death Bunny). In this incarnation, Paul stood, bare, in front of a mirror, deploring the whiteness of his skin and the slackness of his muscles. The Death Bunny lay on the couch and stared at the ceiling. On good days he sat in an armchair and gazed at the floor. When he moved from the couch to the chair, he moved in slow motion. The only activity he engaged in was growing his whiskers. One night, Frances jiggled his shoulder to wake him for supper. "You're alive," said the Death Bunny, shrinking in fright from her contact. As a constant companion, the Tod Hassen gave her no trouble. He made fewer emotional demands than a stone or a cheese. Frances wished the real Paul would return to inhabit his body; while Paul was in hiding, she found she preferred freakish Nip.

As fall turned to winter, Paul's fortunes showed signs of improvement. He left the house carrying a clipboard, and went to long meetings. Frances asked him for names and details. He evaded her questions. When she pressed him too hard, he implied that the meetings were sessions with the pinball machines in a nearby amusement arcade. Frances could stomach large portions of Paul's aggravation; she might well have had more than one stomach, like a milk-giving cow. Often Frances found refuge at the office from Paul's teasing humor; her colleagues at Harwood were cordial, benign and predictable. The men wore their trousers on frontward, and properly zipped. The women were friendly and seemed to think Frances was clever. Both sexes drank water from the cooler out of small paper cups, without gargling the water or threatening to spit it at Frances. When she arrived in the morning and started to work at her desk, she never sat down on a chair daubed with library paste. When she went to collect her belongings at the end of the day, she did not find a soft brown banana in the pocket of her coat. She had come to expect no rude shocks from the Harwood employees, only kindness, good fellowship, loyalty, and pats on the back. Frances was grateful to work in a rational setting, with people who practiced good manners and respected her boundaries. Far be it from her to expect thrills and drama at the office; there was more than enough stimulation in her home life with Paul. Living with an artist breeds a craving for ferment, however; there were days when her work and co-workers seemed servile and bland.

If living with Paul leeched the color from daily existence, then marriage to Paul would estrange her from common humanity. Frances rationed the time she devoted to thinking of marriage, since she knew artists often don't marry, or, if they do, shouldn't. Mate to Paul Treat or a cog in the human collective— was there some third position, some nook reserved only for Frances? At the back of her thoughts was a vision of unconfined spaces, not a niche or retreat, but a wilderness, prairie, or desert; and an image of herself in a noble and lonely vocation—forest ranger, lighthouse keeper, birdbander, goatherd. Or writer? In the dead of the night, when her unconscious mind was unfettered, she had sometimes imagined that writing might be her true destiny. Why else was she editing books? Why else was she Paul Treat's apprentice? She could put down on paper the thoughts she disclosed to no person. She would answer to no one except to herself and her standards. She and Paul could cohabit as equals with dual obsessions. This picture of freedom always ended in a sweat of self-doubt, with Frances aghast at the range of her high-flown presumption. Who was she, unevolved and half-hatched, to lay claim to a destiny? She needed more time watching Paul, learning courage and purpose.

A yearning for solitude, so often peculiar to writers, did not seem to appeal to most writers in Frances's custody. These authors were leery of confinement and fled from their studies. They wrote best, so they claimed, in reading rooms, parks, and cafeterias. Frances had imagined that writers were dreadful misanthropists; but the authors she edited were sociable in the extreme. They telephoned her often and dropped in on her once or twice weekly. If Frances was busy, they tried to spend time with Ruthanne. If Ruthanne shooed them off, they might sit in the lobby reading magazines, or chat with Arlene, the receptionist, as she handled the switchboard. When Frances tried

calling an author, she found the line busy. Authors were as fond
of the telephone as girls in their teens. Frances marveled that
writers were able to finish their manuscripts. Did one hand
write all by itself, like a medium in a trance, while the rest of the
person made phone calls and talked to its friends?

In her three years at Harwood, Frances had known many
writers. Their demands and strange habits had kept her in
training for Paul. Contrasted with Paul, they were merely ec-
centric, not lawless; thus Frances concluded that writers were
not always artists. It was wiser, she felt, to keep her conclusion a
secret, since no one would be happy to hear it, especially her
poet, Matt Bennett. Since Frances's charges might not have been
genuine artists, they nibbled and plucked at their editor, instead
of devouring her. At the end of a given day at the Harwood
Press, she found her skin mostly intact, although one layer thinner. Epidermally speaking, her job was not unduly risky. She
had several years left before she became disincarnate.

Ruthanne had no patience with authors. According to her,
they were monsters of need and dependency. She tried to shield
Frances from calls that were not purely literary, calls relating to
symptoms of illness or the names of astrologers. When Frances
was closeted with a writer for more than an hour, Ruthanne
opened a window, no matter the state of the weather. If Matt
Bennett, the poet of Manhood, came in for a session, Ruthanne
put a bowl of fresh water on top of the bookshelf. When Matt
left, with his boots and his bedroll, she poured out the water, an
old Chinese custom for ridding a dwelling of toxins. After days
filled with sessions, she often looked closely at Frances, like
the owner of a dog who has romped unrestrained in a field. If
Frances had allowed it, she would have gone over her with
tweezers, to extract bits of authors that had fastened themselves
to her hide.

Ruthanne voiced complaints and resentment on Frances's be-
half, so Frances was able to take a mature, balanced viewpoint.
Ruthanne was especially outspoken on the subject of Matt, who
was writing a handbook in verse on male tribal identity. With
his bedroll on his back, Matt made camp in a new place each
night—in the park, on the wharves, or on the floor of a crony's
apartment. One cold morning he was found on a bench in the
Harwood Press mailroom, tucked into his bedroll with two canvas mailbags spread over him. The newscasts reported another
eventful occasion when he stayed in a church after closing and
slept on the altar. Matt had no fixed address, since the Home was
the sphere of the Mother, the Witch Woman working to render
men hairless and knock-kneed. (Ruthanne pointed out that
Matt Bennett himself was quite hairless, a trait caused by genes
from the father's side, never the mother's.) Since the night of his
publicized reading at the Battery Landfill, by the light of a bon-
fire fueled with crates, bedsteads, and siding, Matt had gained
converts who followed him in his migrations, worried men who
hoped sleeping in their clothes would restore their lost maleness.
Some of these men came with Matt when he visited Harwood,
since the offices were heated and equipped with hot water and
telephones. Ruthanne made them cocoa, which contained more
nutrition than coffee. Frances posted their letters and supplied
pens and paper to write them. Matt's men were suspicious of
generous actions from women. They avoided brushing the hand
that brought chocolate or paper. They kept their backs to the
wall and their eyes on the exit. As they crossed her threshold,
Frances noticed them moving their lips, and presumed they
were mouthing a charm or an invocation. She wished she could
reconstruct the magic phrases, but she never caught more than
two words: "dissolve" and "buffalo." Sometimes one of them
left a trail of spicy dust, which had seeped through a hole in the

pocket of his parka. It smelled like nothing found in any kitchen, which was logical, since no spice rack carries witch bane. Ruthanne took offense and stopped dispensing cocoa, but Frances thought Matt might teach her something useful. Perhaps she could master his spells for taming women and utter them in reverse, or with changes of gender. In trying to find a substitute for "buffalo," she wondered if "harpy" would do, or "Atalanta." If she chanted them often on her own home turf, she might reduce the level of Paul's agitation. For that matter, she could direct the chants at Matt, especially during contract negotiations.

Frances had learned in her short career at Harwood that poets are closely related to Hollywood agents. It had come as a shock to overhear their gossip. They talked about money: percentage points, grants, and deals. The old saw about Yankees also applied to poets; they kept cash under floorboards or hidden in the stuffing of mattresses. Rumor had it, a fellow poet had reported, that Matt was the owner of one twelfth of a racehorse. If most poets who passed through her office were closet materialists, the mystery writers she dealt with were shy and unworldly. Frances was in charge of crime and detection at Harwood, since her elders believed that these works did not count as "real" novels. Their opinion was buttressed by the sight of these mystery writers, who were elfin and odd and did not always look like real people. The females of the species resembled cat breeders or fanciers; as it happened, they doted on cats and wore coy, cat-shaped jewelry. They were costumed, not clothed, in disparate, outdated garments: sprays of tulle in their hair, piqué dickeys, and embroidered boleros. They were quite unaware of the fashion, the weather, or the seasons, and might well be caught out in a snowstorm in a clear plastic raincoat. Male crime writers dressed in the daytime for a night at the opera. They were partial to long, swirling scarves, zippered boots, and black capes. These fey, gentle people lived alone or in rooms as paid boarders. They came to see Frances for company as much as for business. As a means of insuring their welcome, they brought gifts of candy, and offered to help with the menial clerical chores. Adelaide Merlin, whose hero was the captain of a vice squad, had damp-dusted the bookshelves while Frances was called to a meeting, and the cloth she had used was her own pink-and-white pocket handkerchief.

Unlike regular writers, who felt Frances owed them her time, the mystery writers believed they should earn her attention. Their dearest delight was a talk about plots and plot elements relating to books they were writing or might write in the future. On a typical day, with Adelaide or one of her kindred, Frances engaged in the loftiest speculation, dealing only with matters of ultimate ethical importance, such as life and death, sin, retribution, and bodies in wardrobes. When discussing a story line, Adelaide would clasp her large handbag; she required something solid to ground her, so great was her fervor. Though her handbag was weighty, she was often compelled to her feet, bouncing and skipping, uplifted by sheer inspiration. Neither author nor editor stayed long in a seated position, so these heated discussions were usually conducted in motion. Ruthanne sometimes joined in, since it made a nice change from her duties, pacing the length of the room and outshouting the others.

"A Ripper plot?" Frances might query.

"Overdone," said Ruthanne. "Done to death."

"One second," answered Adelaide. "I'm thinking. It would work if the Ripper was female."

"A prostitute." Frances waved her pencil. "No, a call girl. It's more hygienic."

"She murders her clients," said Adelaide.

"Would she slash them?" asked Ruthanne. "She's a woman."

"You lose sympathy with slashing," said Frances. "On the other hand, poison is static."

Adelaide was swinging her handbag, with some danger to Frances's jade plant. "Don't get bogged down with the murders. The challenge is in the detection."

Frances thought for a moment. "It's perfect. Finding the link between the victims?"

"I love it," said Adelaide, pirouetting. "I love driving Captain Sparks crazy."

"Watch out for the lamp," said Ruthanne. "Make the captain be one of her clients."

"Your readers would hate it," said Frances. "You got mail when you broke his engagement."

"That's a thought," answered Adelaide. "I'll use it. Not a lapse, just a steamy temptation."

"Take Sparks out of vice," added Frances. "It's time you promoted him to homicide."

Ruthanne stooped to pick up some papers, blown down during Adelaide's gyrations. "Do I get a vote?" she demanded. "Promote him without Sergeant Cooney."

At the end of these brainstorming meetings, which would end as abruptly as they started, the editor, the assistant, and the author were as flushed as three dancers after a workout. Hammy Griner poked his head in the door late one morning. Observing the scene, he looked stricken. "You're enjoying yourselves," he admonished. Hammy worked with the glossier authors, whose names were the staples of book clubs. These journalists, biographers, and critics served on juries and made reputations. Hammy often passed wry, mocking comments on the oddity of Frances's clients. Hammy hid when Matt came to the office, since he feared Matt might try to recruit him. He feared Adelaide, too, or her clothes, which he thought needed cleaning and pressing. "I can't talk to your people," said Hammy. "They make me feel stodgy." Hammy's people, by contrast, made Frances feel rowdy and freakish. With these authors, dressed in suits, vests, and neckties, who might have been bankers, she found slang and unladylike oaths on the tip of her tongue. In the eyes of the world, Frances melted right into the background, although being a towhead had brought her unwelcome attention. She herself was not odd—or, at least to her knowledge, exceptional; but she knew odd was better, and rare birds made far sweeter music. Leonardo da Vinci was odd, since he thought men could fly. Saints were odd, without doubt; no plain man claims to gossip with angels. Her own Paul was odd, too; oddness went hand in hand with his talent. Did Hammy dread talent as much as he dreaded strange people? If so, reasoned Frances, then Hammy was in the wrong business. Hammy rarely read fiction. He preferred books by men who explained things. As an editor, he closed open questions and tied up loose ends. "You ought to like mysteries," said Frances. "They come with solutions." "I can't stand suspense," Hammy said. "I don't like being fooled with."

Life fooled with you, whether you wished it or Hammy denied it. Life was full of sly hints and stray clues with disquieting undertones. All was not as it seemed, in spite of broad smiles or bright sunshine. When you walked in the woods, stepping briskly and humming a ditty, the dead log you tripped on might well be a moldering body. If you trusted the surface and walked with your head lifted skyward, you would miss the small patch of slick ice partly covered by leaves. The suspense in crime stories was temperate—if not soporific—compared to suspense in real life, which supplied no catharsis. Suspense in crime novels moved forward, directed by logic. The suspense line in life was not straight; it was wavy or crooked. Life with Paul, for example, was a cliff-hanger, filled with uncertainty. Paul himself was a mystery, as was his connection with Frances. Loving Paul was like swimming in a quarry too deep to be sounded, lined with outcroppings jutting forth sharply and fatal to divers. Most people were riddles, but they yielded their secret in time. Their secret, for the most part, was only the sum of their habits. Whether musing or resting, his face and his body in repose, Paul Treat was a caldron of secrets, of thoughts behind thoughts. Frances paid no attention to the thoughts Hammy might be concealing, though his round, whiskered face wore expressions of constant unrest. At home, she kept watch over Paul like a student seismologist who fears the least waver of the needle or scratch on the drum.

Paul had been dormant for nearly three weeks at a stretch, although dormant in Paul's terms was active—in fact, hyperactive. He went out before breakfast and often returned after dinner. With Paul in high gear, there was no conversation between them, but Frances deduced he was close to a source of new funds. The suicide play had been bound between black cardboard covers; stacks of copies were piled on Paul's desk, as were copies of the budget. Paul sat up at night sorting résumés from actors and stagehands. In one intimate exchange, he asked Frances to brush his good suit. All these clues added up to a backer in hand or in view, as did Paul's collection of matchbooks from elegant restaurants. On the face of the evidence, Frances had a case, and a good one, except for some interesting data that did not fit neatly. Why was Paul carrying a book on heredity in his briefcase? Or an article concerning the genetic transmission of genius? How was the theory of genetics related to suicide? Was Paul bent on proving that suicide ran in the family? Perhaps he had studied the subject and reached the conclusion that suicides were geniuses and geniuses were earmarked for suicide. The reader may wonder why Frances engaged in detection when she could have asked Paul direct questions and got some straight answers. Straight answers from Paul had the power to increase her anxieties. What she got was not "straight" as in "honest," but "straight" as in "straight between the eyes." Paul never divulged his thought processes, just his decisions. He never gave answers; he issued pronouncements or edicts. Frances had learned to postpone these dire moments of reckoning. One direct question might turn her whole world on its head.

The evidence mounted, and the evidence boded good fortune. Paul bought a new suit and a watch that told time under water. He subscribed to a service that picked up his telephone messages, and a paper that ran daily listings of box-office profits. He asked Frances to call him at night during meetings or dinners, to convince his companions that other producers were wooing him. Since success bred success, he hooked up a sunlamp in the bathroom; a tan in midwinter is not a criterion of failure. There was hope in the air and a side of smoked salmon in the icebox. Paul never drank spirits, but he ordered lime soda by the case. Once again he exhibited a personal interest in Frances, or at least in her tenderest tissues and undermost areas. After such a long drought, Paul was ardent as well as ingenious. With Frances for his exercise mat, he was spry as a primate. The Act of Darkness promoted physical fitness; Frances soon found her wind was improving as well as her balance. In some ways these workouts were more scientific than amorous. Paul seemed to set store by the depth and the angle of entry. Since Paul was so diligent, Frances began to conjecture that she might be his choice as the channel for transmitting genius. (A girl prodigy, sprung from her womb, would be short and flat-chested; she was glad, nonetheless, that her genes might have earned Paul's acceptance.)

Major cycles of sexual bounty had one of two meanings: Paul

was close to the end of his tether or else optimistic. Every sign seemed to point to the latter, and one sign in particular. Paul had given his bees to the Roosevelt Botanical Gardens. When the weather was cold, bees would sometimes get in, seeking warmth. Drugged with heat, they might settle on the arms of a chair or the carpet. Drowsy as they were, they delivered a powerful sting, right through Frances's sleeves, or her socks if she went without shoes. The bees had worked hard for their food when they lived on the fire escape. Their chief source of nectar was the parks, where the plant life was sooty. In their home amid beds of exotics, they would sting her no longer. Paul was eating rich foods nowadays, like his hardworking bees. Since his diet had improved, perhaps he would not sting her either.

With these notions in mind, Frances eased herself out of Paul's grasp, disengaging their arms and their legs and their centers of pleasure. Paul muttered at Frances's desertion and tried to restrain her; he was sluggish and weak, like a python digesting a rodent. Frances went to the kitchen and got out a plate and a tray. She assembled the ingredients for Paul's favorite three-decker sandwich: anchovies, peanut butter, lettuce, and Limburger cheese; pumpernickel, cucumber, mayonnaise, and optional onion. When she brought back the tray, Paul raised himself on one elbow. He inspected its contents, then fastened his eyes on her haunches. He seemed to be waging a lengthy internal debate about which would slip down with less effort, the sandwich or Frances. Paul chose the sandwich, since Frances did not come with onions. He ate quickly, with small, dainty bites, and made noises of happiness. With Paul so contented, Frances abandoned all caution.

"Is it settled?" she asked. "Did they put up the money? Who are they?"

"Not a fortune," said Paul. "They're a middle-aged woman with a trust fund."

"An amateur? How did you find her? Are you sure she won't meddle?"

"I have total control," answered Paul. "We start casting on Monday."

Frances bounced up and down on the bed in an outburst of glee.

"Cut it out," complained Paul. "I'll get seasick. I want you to quit."

"You have only to ask," answered Frances, and kissed his right foot.

"Not my feet!" shouted Paul. "Watch it, Frances! My feet are off limits!"

"Love knows no limits," said Frances, and grabbed for the left one.

Paul was frightened of feet, which he claimed had a life of their own. He had laid down a rule that all love play stop short at the ankles. Once, Frances had succeeded in nipping Paul's penis with her toes. She tried it again, but Paul pinned her down on the mattress. In the scuffle that ensued, Frances squashed the last morsel of sandwich.

"Let me go," panted Frances. "I'll be good. I've got cheese on my elbow."

"You went for my jewels," grumbled Paul.

"My feet made me do it."

Paul sat up and released her. He covered his parts with his hands. Then he covered himself with the tray, for extra protection.

"No more tricks," ordered Paul. "Back to business. Let's settle your quitting."

"Quitting," she repeated. She brushed crusts of bread off the covers. She plumped up the pillows and tucked in the blanket and sheets.

"Stop fussing," said Paul. He tugged at the top of the blanket. "I need you to help with the casting. That gives you a week."

Frances folded the quilt. She stood very still, looking upward, as if she were listening to a broadcast from Pluto or Saturn. At first the emission was muted and broken by static; then the message came through loud and clear, forcing Frances to hear it. In moments of crisis, Frances chose flight over combat. She poised for retreat, like an animal sensing a predator.

"When you're not taking notes," Paul went on, "you can work on the costumes."

"No," she said, stalling. "I hate sewing. I never could sew."

"The budget is tight," answered Paul. "You have to pitch in."

"I can't," whispered Frances.

"All right, don't!" Paul was growing impatient. "You can help paint the sets. Or do props. Find me parts from wrecked cars."

Frances lacked practice in pitting her will against Paul's. Paul made requests in the name of higher values. "No" was a word that rarely escaped her lips; refusal could prove more costly than compliance. If Frances refused him, how would Paul perceive her? As the enemy of art and man's best aspirations? In her own little way, she did her bit for art; she worked for writers and fostered their ambitions. Where Paul was concerned, she had an established record. An efficiency expert, studying Frances's schedule, would have to conclude that Paul was her real employer. Only forty hours in her week belonged to Harwood; one hundred and twenty-eight belonged to Paul. What did Paul want? Dear God, what did Paul want? She felt like the map of Europe as seen by Napoleon, with every country invaded except for England.

Frances was naked. Her nakedness lacked distinction. In order to give her statement weight and value, she draped a blanket around her like a toga. Paul was cleaning his toenails, using the tines of a fork. He dug too deep and gave a yelp of anger.

"Please listen," begged Frances. "I don't want to quit. I love Harwood."

"Suit yourself," said Paul. He rubbed the offended toe. He bent the fork and shaped it into a circle. "You're a very strange person, Frances. Why didn't you say so?"

Life with an artist is training for living alone. It is also good practice for living with more than one person. An artist belongs to his work, not to his sweetheart. His work shares their space, like a roomer with kitchen privileges. Paul's suicide play had outgrown their crowded lodgings and moved to the Center Street Theatre. Since Paul was joined to his play at the hip and the navel, Frances went down to the theatre in order to see him. The suicide play had expanded to fill its new quarters, like a goldfish transferred from a bowl to an outdoor pond. It grew fatter from scene to scene and act to act, ingesting large groups of players, non-speaking and speaking. It seemed to derive its substance from Paul's own body, sucking fat from his cheeks and muscle tone out of his torso. Directing the suicide play was a form of suicide. By opening night, Paul Treat might be a shadow but the play would be sleek and resplendent and surging with blood cells. As the play grew in scale, it also grew in genius, fed as it was by the steady drip of Paul's vital fluids. It was less of a suicide play than a suicide circus, a magic show, macabre and vaudevillian. Jugglers displayed the instruments of self-murder: daggers, revolvers, and barbers' straight-edged razors. Sword-swallowers swallowed glass, coins, bolts, and crosses. Acrobats leapt from platforms or dangled from nooses. Act II, Scene 2 portrayed the exceptional cases, daft or creative attempts, unique in the annals. Paul had imported magicians to stage these illusions: the boy who sawed through his neck with a hacksaw; the man who drove nails into his skull with a blacksmith's hammer; and the woman who drowned, upside down, in a bucket of water.

Frances attended every evening rehearsal, carrying a satchel of token work from Harwood. Down at the theatre, surrounded by unionized experts, she wondered why Paul had imagined he needed her services. During each break, she offered her help to the staff, who turned her down flat or invented small jobs to appease her. Once in a while, the stage manager sent her for coffee or the costume designer allowed her to give him a neck rub. When the assistant director knocked over a box full of paper clips, Frances fell to her knees and proved her good will by retrieving them. Competing with Frances for marginal or amateur employment were various unknown volunteers, who had snared the best jobs. Several nights in a row, a woman in a hat took Paul's notes. This woman was replaced by another one, with long hair and glasses. One night Frances took notes. She noticed a third volunteer, a tall, wide-hipped woman with a chignon, who was cuing the actors. Frances wore glasses herself, for distance and driving. She found them at the bottom of her satchel and set them on her nose. One earpiece was broken and the lenses were spotted and streaky, but Frances could see that the three volunteers were one person. Using her glasses as a kind of outlandish lorgnette, Frances also observed that this person possessed some authority. The lighting director hailed her and showed her a diagram. The wardrobe mistress approached her and gave her a cashbox.

An elbow nudged Frances in the ribs. Paul snatched at her

Hillyer, like Frances, was working to further Paul's
Kip Hillyer was Paul's benefactress, and therefore her

hearsals wore on, Frances found herself banished to the
s. She had nothing to do, and her lack of employment
rassed her. The costume designer brought his dog, a toy
e, to the theatre. Asleep in his basket, the dog had more
ose than Frances. The costume designer supplied his pet
dle with biscuits. He took her for walks and stooped over to
tle her topknot. Frances's presence went largely unnoticed by
ul, unless she dozed off in her chair or began to read manu-
ripts. Confined to her seat, she had time to watch Paul watch
Kip Hillyer. During run-throughs he gave more attention to
Kip than to his actors. He seemed finely attuned to each change
in expression or gesture, a difficult task, since Kip's face was by
nature expressionless. If she happened to yawn, he leaned over
and questioned her urgently, forgetting that yawning was normal as the hour approached midnight. If she shifted position or
stretched out a kink in her neck, Paul called for a break and
asked someone to bring her an aspirin. Riding home in the taxi
with Frances, he reviewed the day's progress, recalling improvements or setbacks from Kip Hillyer's viewpoint: "Kip thinks we
should find a replacement for Melanie Lambert." "Kip agrees
that the Ferris wheel works if we move it upstage." Kip this, Kip
that, Kip paste-it-in-your hat, thought Frances, who found that
this ditty restrained her from making rude comments. She had
frequent occasion to murmur this useful refrain, since the name
of Kip Hillyer was never too far from Paul's lips. Paul's behavior
caused Frances anxiety as well as resentment. In the days before
Kip, Paul ignored or insulted his backers. The reversal of roles
between artist and patron was wrong; it was up to the patron to
humble herself to the artist.

clipboard. "Did you ge̶̶ ̶
you didn't, you've had it.̶

"Who's that lady?" aske̶

"I thought so. You took th̶

"Over there," pursued Fran̶
her some money."

"Kip Hillyer," said Paul. "Can̶
terrible."

Since Paul was aggrieved, Frances̶
profile. She took notes in a round, childis̶
more censure. When Paul left his seat to ̶
strate blocking, she kept the elusive Kip H̶
surveillance. Miss Hillyer, or Mrs., took a se̶
the theatre. She followed the action on stage w̶
script. She made marks on the script and pasted ̶
pages. When the actors were resting, she appeared̶
out bank checks. Even a novice detective on he̶
stakeout would be forced to conclude that Kip H̶
Paul's unnamed backer, the "middle-aged woman with̶
fund," to use Paul's own phrasing. Frances believed in the̶
fund. The signs were explicit: the coat with a rip in the seam,̶
absence of jewelry; the comfortable shoes with scuffed toes; t̶
plaid Scottish kilt. When applied to Kip Hillyer, however,
"middle-aged" was a spurious description, unless you computed
the term of her life span at seventy. Her person showed signs of
neglect, but no signs of decay. Kip Hillyer was older than Frances by five or six years. She was plainer than Frances, but her
plainness was akin to her shoes, a cover designed to protect her
from classification. To Frances, who was practiced in hiding her
light under bushels, these tactics did not seem demure, but con-
trived and deceitful. Frances was briefly ashamed of her bristly
responses. Why was she casting Kip Hillyer in the role of her

rival? Kip̶
interests.̶
own.

As re̶
sidelin̶
emba̶
poodl̶
purp̶
poo̶
ruf̶
P̶
s̶

By the start of the third week, Kip Hillyer had grown more exacting. She telephoned Paul late at night to propose new ideas. She telephoned Paul on days off and requested long meetings. She pre-empted Paul's dinners and began to make inroads on breakfast. When the telephone rang and Frances was the person who answered, Kip asked for Paul Treat as if she were calling an office. When Frances complained, Paul referred to Kip's pitiful childhood. She had lost both her parents before she had cut her first tooth. A succession of guardians had met their reward, like her parents, leaving nine-year-old Kip to be raised by an elderly servant. Perhaps these sad facts explained her reliance on Paul, since directors are classic authority figures, like fathers. Kip's telephone calls were no longer concerned with the theatre. Paul was summoned to deal with domestic and psychic emergencies. One Sunday she discovered a water bug the size of a grapefruit taking his ease in the soap dish attached to her bathtub. On and off, for a week, she heard footsteps that crisscrossed the roof. A man, who might well have been one of her telephone breathers, followed her into the subway and stared at her bosoms. Most recently, Paul had been wakened at four in the morning by a weeping Kip Hillyer who threatened to cut off her hair. "Let her," said Frances, who was not at her best before breakfast. "She could hurt herself, Frances," said Paul as he sped on his errand.

The art of detection is a mixture of insight and logic. Logic suggested that Paul and Kip Hillyer were lovers. From a logical standpoint, Frances had cause to be jealous, but try as she might, she felt only confusion and pique. Being jealous of Paul was a useless and laughable notion; it was as if Isaac Newton had been jealous of the forces of gravity, or the oceans believed that they governed the phases of the moon. No woman who mates with an artist can own him entirely; she is lucky to get him on a yearly

renewable lease. Frances made a game effort to imagine Paul
mating with Kip, to see if the picture would stir up unbearable
feelings. She tried to envision their coupling in graphic detail: in
and out, up and down, back and forth, back to front, side by
side. Her effort was a failure: Kip Hillyer stayed clothed, as did
Paul, like a girl doll and a boy doll whose garments were painted
on their bodies. Intuition told Frances that Paul did not act like a
lover. A lover would be sly and forgetful; Paul was rattled and
eager to please. Sexual fidelity was a lot to expect from an artist,
since artists required a rich diet of varied experience. When Paul
was unfaithful he would not choose the likes of Kip Hillyer,
whose hair was so drab, while Frances was as blonde as a jon-
quil. Whatever bound Paul to Kip Hillyer was stranger than
sex; unless, of course, Frances was bent on denying the obvious.

Frances needed a rest from her thoughts, which were ruining
her sleep. During meetings at Harwood, she dozed without
closing her eyes. Ruthanne believed Frances was suffering from
faulty nutrition, and brought her yeast tablets dissolved in a glass
of tomato juice. Frances swallowed the yeast; but Gus Stafford
was better than vitamins. Augustus ("Gus") Stafford was a
prize-winning mystery novelist, a man of great honor who declined to accept his awards. Judges and critics delivered the same
solemn verdict: Gus had turned mysteries into a genuine art
form. Gus Stafford wrote novels that dealt with the problem of
evil. His murderers were plagued with a conscience; his detec-
tives disliked playing God. At the climax, the latter gave the gift
of free choice to the former; the sound of the killer's own pistol
rang out from off stage. Gus blurred the line between felons and
servants of justice. His victims were tarred with the same shade
of guilt as his culprits. He was writing a book that was set in a
Catholic convent, a departure for Gus, since he rarely placed
women in the foreground. As his editor, Frances had given him

some valuable pointers regarding the gift for disinterested
friendship in females. Since his wife had deserted him, Gus had
been wary of women. His wife was an actress with a yearning
for personal glory. Gus had wanted to prevent her from degrad-
ing her art and her talent. He had tried to convince her that
work was its own best reward. She had paid for her sins, although Gus took no pleasure in saying so: Mrs. Stafford found
fame as the girl in the nose-drop commercials. Both Frances and
Gus had been orphaned, in a sense, by the theatre. She esteemed
him for keeping a chivalrous face on his sorrows, such a grave,
handsome face, with its well-modeled profile and jawline. From
what she could tell, she had earned his respect in return. No
other writer had ever acknowledged her services. *The Sisterhood
Murders* was dedicated to Frances Girard.

Gus Stafford was full of good values, like bread made with
whole grains and seeds. Frances found herself scheduling extra
appointments with him, and using these meetings as doses of
moral refreshment. At the end of a day, when they finished their
line-by-line editing, Gus began asking Frances to join him for
coffee and a sandwich. At first, Frances ate and drank quickly
and rushed to the theatre; then she lingered and chewed her
food slowly, which helped her digestion. She arrived at rehearsals half an hour late, then an hour. Her absence was no more
significant than her attendance. When rehearsal was over, she
had always met Paul in the lobby, but for several nights running,
he left and forgot to collect her. Later, Paul was contrite, but he
told her to get home without him; he needed the time after
hours to calm panicky actors. One evening Gus Stafford asked
Frances to eat a real dinner, several courses with wine in a restaurant with cloths on the tables. She saw no good reason for
declining this kind invitation. She could skip one rehearsal with
a record of sitting through twenty.

Dining with Gus was a novel experience for Frances. She had picked up a lot of bad habits from eating with Paul. She finished her soup before Gus had dispatched the first mouthful. She found herself watching the level of broth in the soup bowl; the level dropped slowly, since he laid down his spoon between sips. When the lobster arrived, Frances went for the claws and the tail, courting sure disappointment by eating the choicest parts first. Gus Stafford ate lobster the way he conducted his life, with the rare self-command born of wisdom earned slowly and painfully. He began with the small legs of the lobster, which add up to eight, sucking meat, but more air, through the pencil-thin tubular shells. He spooned out the coral, which Frances had downed in one bite. He chopped it and added the mince to his hot melted butter. Delaying his pleasure, he next went to work on the body, finding minuscule shreds of good meat between the tough feathers. If this were his birthday and the lobster a gift to be opened, Gus would smooth out the wrappings, refold them, and wind up the ribbon, and then, only then, would he let himself look at his present. In the matter of opening gifts there were two kinds of people: savers, like Gus, and rippers and tearers, like Frances.

Gus had finished his meal and was ready to make conversation. He looked proud and contented, aware he had given his utmost, just as he looked when he turned in his recent book manuscript. Like a child who loves hearing the same story over and over, Frances asked him to tell her why writers should never give interviews, and why they should stay underground till their character is formed. "Do you read your reviews?" Frances asked, though she knew Gus's answer. Gus did not read reviews; he kept every one in a big box, waiting under his bed while he grew in detachment and balance. Gus believed, with the sages of China, in conducting his triumphs like a funeral.

This maxim held true in reverse, but Gus had no reason for testing it. Since his books were successful, his behavior was doomed to be sober. It was Frances's duty, as his editor, to urge Gus to help with publicity. When their coffee arrived, she brought up the question of photographs. Would Gus allow Harwood to feature his picture on the jacket? "My work has to stand on its own," answered Gus in refusal. Gus compared writing books to a child making toy paper boats. Once the vessel is launched with a prayer on a current of water, neither author nor child can insure that the craft will stay upright. Alone among artists, Gus Stafford was free from ambition. Most artists, like Paul, had to wrestle the fearsome beast daily. Frances was honored that Gus seemed to wish for her friendship. Too rarely did editors make friends with authors they cared for. Many authors saw editors as maids-of-all-work or valets; others perceived them as governesses, tutors, or wardens. Gus gave Frances her due as an equal; he neither exploited nor feared her. If the truth can be told, Frances felt more at ease as a menial. Being equals with Gus was a burden as well as an honor; she might lose his respect if they differed on matters of dogma.

Gus kissed Frances good night as a friend may embrace a fond friend, mouth to mouth, with closed lips, but applying no unlawful pressure. Frances walked taller from having spent time in his presence, from breathing his air, and from being exposed to sound principles. She had once read a survey compiled by a group of psychiatrists, a comparison of artists with subjects in normal professions. The artists they tested scored higher in psychopathology, and especially high in antisocial behavior. Gus Stafford's example would puzzle these worthy clinicians, who believed people labeled "creative" can never be virtuous. As Frances ascended the five flights of stairs to Paul's loft, she resolved to bring order and harmony into their lives.

Paul might learn, if she taught him, to view mere events in perspective, and human endeavor as God or a jet pilot sees it, as the movement of dust motes, dark specks on a flat, colored surface. Every play Paul directed was like a casino roulette game, with Fate as the croupier and Paul as a desperate gambler risking all of his chips on one spin of the wheel and one number. Paul could profit from heeding Gus Stafford on growing through failure; every artist, said Gus, gains humility from his mistakes.

Filled with zeal, like a pastor appointed to preach to the savages, Frances opened the door on a scene that would test her vocation. The lights were ablaze. The bedspread was littered with clothing. A suitcase lay open on the floor, strewn with female apparel. Paul was not at the theatre, displaying exemplary patience, persuading tired actors to rise to undreamed-of achievements. Paul was emptying drawers, tossing garments over his shoulder: some landed on the bed; others fell in a heap in the suitcase; a blouse and a knee sock had draped themselves over a lampshade. Frances crept up behind him, afraid for herself and her wardrobe. Paul had found a chemise, powder blue, trimmed with insets of lace. He crumpled it, stretched it, and tugged it between his fists. Paul turned around. The chemise caught her full in the face.

"It better be good!" shouted Paul, flinging nightgowns and headscarves. "It better be medical. I don't see you bleeding or limping!"

Frances lowered her eyes, clasped her hands, and endured the eruption. Very soon she resembled a clothesline left out in a whirlwind. Compared to most women, her personal possessions were limited. Unless Paul began to throw shoes, he had run out of missiles.

"Don't come near me!" yelled Paul, a request she was pleased to comply with. He slammed the drawers shut and aimed a swift kick at the suitcase. In spite of his anger, she saw he was very near weeping. He was wrinkling his nostrils and pinching the bridge of his nose, as if he were quelling a sneeze during church or a concert. He collapsed in the armchair. His bulk was contained on three sides. Frances drew nearer, but kept a low bookcase between them.

"I don't need this," said Paul. "I can't handle a personal crisis."

"What crisis?" asked Frances. "Did something go wrong at the theatre?"

"My career is at stake," muttered Paul. "I need a calm mind."

Frances approached him, appalled by the flow of real tears. She stood by his chair. It seemed safe, so she reached down and touched him.

Paul flinched at her touch. He covered his face with his forearm. "Why couldn't you wait? Why couldn't you wait till we opened?"

"Wait for what?" implored Frances.

"Where were you?" said Paul. "No. Don't tell me."

Frances relaxed. Paul was harboring jealous suspicions. She felt guilt and remorse. She had tampered with Paul's concentration. When Paul was directing a play, his composure was vital. Was it she who was jealous? Had she struck a low blow at Paul's art? When he heard she'd had dinner with Gus, he would come to his senses. After all, he referred to Gus Stafford as "pious" and "tight-assed."

When Paul heard she'd had dinner with Gus, he rose up from the armchair. His fists were clenched and the look on his face was not friendly. Frances measured the distance between them (two feet and some inches). Instead of retreating or flinching, she held her position.

"Dinner?" said Paul. "Or box lunch?" His face was a study: a compound of menace conflicting with rank curiosity.

"You have dinner with Kip," Frances said, trading challenge for challenge.

"Did you come?" questioned Paul. He was taking his pulse in two places, at the vein on the side of his neck and the vein on his temple.

Frances stared at him. Paul was a great one for sexual motives. He believed that a man and a woman, alone in a room, will have sex just as surely as smoke is a warning of fire. She had always kept thinker and theory in separate compartments, forgetting that theories reflected the theorist's nature. The partition between the compartments gave way in an instant. She knew beyond doubt that Paul reasoned from special experience. Frances did badly at card games. Her face was too mobile. She played just as poorly in contests of love and diplomacy. Paul could read her expressions before she had ordered her thoughts, and before she had chosen to speak them or leave them unspoken.

"I don't want to deal with this, Frances." Paul turned toward the window.

"You might as well tell me," said Frances. "Or I'll ask direct questions."

"I did a bad thing," answered Paul.

"I don't blame you," said Frances.

"It's worse than you think," Paul explained.

"Do you love her?" asked Frances.

She tugged at his elbow. He left her and went to the window. He blew on the glass, making circles of steam on the pane. He traced lines in the circles and lines through the lines, forming X's. He rubbed out the lines and began blowing circles again.

"She looked up my clippings," said Paul. This time he drew crosses. "She went to the newspaper files and she read all about me."

"Your reviews," Frances urged, "and your interviews. She's an investor."

Paul's behavior alarmed her. Was he feeling the strain of his schedule? Was he losing his grip after nights without adequate sleep?

"She approved of my genes," Paul went on. "She decided on me. She had picked a black actor but he had notched ears and one kidney."

Frances approached him. At last Paul consented to face her. She took both his hands, which were hot. Was he running a fever?

"She made me get tested," said Paul. "The black actor was sterile."

Frances tilted her head. She banged on her skull with her palm, like a swimmer who tries to release water trapped in her ear. She heard noise from the street down below, honking horns and dogs barking. Her hearing was fine, but her heart had sustained an impairment.

"Do you still get the money," she asked, "if she can't have a baby?"

"She might be too old," answered Paul. "Close to forty it's harder."

While he spoke, Paul's eyes widened as if in acute disbelief, like an innocent party arrested and tried on false evidence. He seemed to place Frances in the role of defending attorney, who needed to know the whole truth to obtain his acquittal.

"She uses a timer. She makes me stay in for ten minutes. She lies on her back for an hour with her legs in the air."

Frances tried to recoil. She tried to display proper horror. Paul had betrayed her and every known code of morality. She must make a gesture that signified disapprobation. A woman deceived must take action or bear full complicity.

"I'm a piece of salami," said Paul. His pose was dejected. His shoulders were bent and he carried his hands as if shackled. Frances resisted an impulse to mop Paul's poor forehead. The tables were turned, showing Paul more tormented than sinning: surely she was the victim and Paul was the double-dyed villain?

"I did it for my art," uttered Paul. "But I have to be punished."

"Straighten up," ordered Frances. "You can't let the play be a failure."

"Get me out of this, Frances," said Paul. He looked at her sideways. From his glance she could tell he believed the rough weather was over. Frances, his Sancho, would follow him through mud and quagmire while the villagers catcalled and pelted their backs with spoiled cabbages. She moved to the bureau. She turned and looked Paul in the eye.

"You get out of it," Frances instructed. "But you can't live with me while you do it."

For the second time that night, drawers were emptied and suitcases filled. The belongings were Paul's, though he borrowed the luggage from Frances. Like a faithful retainer, she saw to the folding and packing, stuffing tissue in the arms of his jackets and rolling his neckties. She remembered his bathrobe, his shaving equipment and nailbrush, and included a box of green gumdrops, his favorite candy. She had the impression of sending her firstborn to camp, and was tempted to tuck in a few stamped and self-addressed postcards. She picked up the suitcase and lugged it as far as the door. In fact, Paul resembled a child; he looked fretful and homesick. Frances opened the door, but he dawdled at the edge of the threshold.

"She can't cook," he began. "She puts gingersnap crumbs in the pot roast. . . ."

"Here is your key ring," said Frances. "I'm keeping your house keys."

Frances took Paul by the elbow and led him outside. Before he could finish his speech, she ran back to the loft. She bolted the door, which was guaranteed fireproof and soundproof. Paul's last words filtered through nonetheless: "She leaves hair in the bathtub."

Any heroine worthy of print is aware of her mission. She endures every trial with the knowledge that she has been chosen. In the eyes of the world she appears to be modest and wrenlike; in her own heart of hearts she is fitted with sword, shield, and armor. St. Catherine displaying the wheel that had broken her body was no prouder than Frances of the wrongs she had gallantly suffered. Saints die for God, whereas Frances was martyred for art. Like the saints, Frances never cried out or cast blame on her torturers. Far be it from her to entertain vengeance or spite, such as ordering a coffin and having it sent to Kip's house, or lying in ambush for Paul as he left for the theatre, having coated the pavement with grease used to lubricate motors. She and Paul were both joined in a cause that was greater than either; she wished him the best and she hoped that his enterprise prospered. She kept her chin high as she walked through the hallways of Harwood, lit up from inside by her pain and her courage in stifling it. In the eyes of her colleagues she read new regard and approval. Her dignified carriage elicited interesting comments. Hammy Griner observed that she'd grown several inches in height; Ruthanne Marvin inquired whether Frances had need of a neck rub.

For days, Frances lived in a state of exquisite transcendence, as if she had filled a prescription for strong analgesics. Like an engine in overdrive, Frances worked hard with no effort. She soothed ruffled authors; and accepted a prize for Gus Stafford, who signed the check over to an outfit called Pen Pals for Prisoners. When Adelaide Merlin came down with a case of pneumonia, Frances went by every evening to cook her a meal. Frances visited her aunt, who was caring for Lewis, the cat; and startled her badly by painting the porch and the lawn chairs. Ruthanne sprained her ankle and Frances took over the typing. "It's my foot, not my wrist," said Ruthanne. "Leave me something to do." "It's my pleasure," said Frances, who also took over the filing. "You look sick," said Ruthanne, "and you're acting extremely peculiar."

Who can say where her zeal might have led her, unchecked by Paul Treat? She might have left Harwood and entered divinity school. It is likelier still that she might have developed a skin rash, an unexplained patch of eruptions related to nerves. Every impulse toward service is tainted by personal motives, and Frances's spate of good works was both brief and impure. Her generous acts were intended to answer a question: How could Paul, how could he, forsake a fine person like her? As time passed, she grew wretched and glum and inclined to self-pity. Her devotion to others did not withstand Paul's daily calls. These telephone calls were dramatic and often inaudible, since he spoke in a whisper or over the roar of the traffic. He was forced to sneak out to a telephone booth on the corner, or call from a room in Kip's house when he thought she was sleeping. The audible part of Paul's messages carried scant comfort; he seemed to believe Frances needed to share his experience.

"I'm frightened," Paul told her. "She says Mohawk Indians ate dogmeat."

"I don't want to hear this," said Frances.

"It makes sperm swim faster."

"I'm going to hang up," Frances warned.

"That's not all," whispered Paul. "We have to breathe tur-
pentine fumes and drink egg white and garlic."

"That's it!" shouted Frances. "Don't call me!"

"I'm dying," Paul answered.

These short conversations, and others of similar kidney, gave
Frances a fine sense of grievance and righteous resentment. Any
court in the land would uphold her entitlement to outrage: Paul
persisted in error without giving proof of contrition. The mantle
of anger fit better than the trappings of sainthood, although
Frances was frequently hobbled by pangs of compassion. In
order to harden her heart, she wrapped anger around her and
went forth like a pilgrim to canvass her friends and relations.

Edie Childs was the first on her list: Edie hated Paul Treat.
The feeling was mutual, but Paul's grounds were purely aes-
thetic: "Your friend has no neck," he declared, "not to mention
fat ankles." After one fatal dinner *chez* Childs, lit by stubs of red
candles, which Paul had referred to out loud as "the dog dicks of
Liège," Frances and Edie had never exchanged social visits, pre-
ferring to meet at a restaurant for luncheon or coffee. Edie did
charity work with disturbed adolescents, teaching them reading
and writing and personal hygiene. She had taken a general
course in abnormal psychology, and classified Paul as incipiently
sociopathic. Frances confided in Edie at the Woman's Guild
tearoom, over cheese toasts with watercress salad and miniature
cupcakes. Her tale aroused Edie's attention as well as her appetite; she doubled her order of cheese toasts and added beet
aspic. She ate the corn relish and finished the watermelon pick-
les, explaining that Paul lacked a conscience, like a child who is
born mute or blind. As she warmed to her topic, she ate both
their portions of cupcakes. She predicted the bleakest of futures
unless Frances pulled up her socks. Drunkards or gamblers, she
stated, would make better lovers than Paul. There were organi-

zations that helped people deal with compulsions, but no social
agency aided the morally void. By the end of their luncheon,
Frances felt as grim as her future. "I've told you and told you,"
said Edie, "and you know how I hate being right."

Next on her list Frances interviewed Gloria Cohen, who
wrote funny novels that needed a minimum of editing. Gloria
was brisk and reclusive. She lived by herself. "You'll have to
come here," she announced. "I hate leaving the house." Gloria
went out once a year to her dentist and doctor. She arranged
with the market to have all her groceries delivered. She collected
the cookbooks of every state, region, and nation, but she hated to
cook and ate foods that were frozen or canned. When her novels
were published, she agreed to do readings in bookshops; she did
not go to plays, and did not know Paul's works or renown. Her
apartment was furnished, but she slept, ate, and wrote in her
bed. Her bed also served as an armchair when Frances came
calling. She dressed in a nightshirt and wore woolen socks on
her feet, which had poor circulation since Gloria used them so
rarely. Frances admired her for paring her life to the bone, for
needing so little from others and keeping her own counsel. Se-
cluded or not, she was wise in the ways of the world; she gave
the impression of having renounced a great love. Like most
satirists, Gloria was kinder to persons than groups; people in
herds were her target, not lone individuals. Frances never knew
what to expect from disclosure to Gloria. Her reactions were
bracing, original, and always impartial.

Gloria got up out of bed during Frances's recital. As she listened, she did a few knee bends and full Yogic neck rolls. She
stretched toward the ceiling, bent over, and reached for her toes.
She was limber and loose for a girl with an invalid's habits, but
she started to pant and her forehead was covered with moisture.
Frances stopped talking. She felt she should make an apology.

"Am I watching your regular workout or is it my story?"

"I admit," agreed Gloria, "it lacks soporific ingredients."

"Come back to bed," pleaded Frances.

"I'll sit," answered Gloria. "The last time I sat in this chair was in nineteen-aught-seventy."

"I'll get you some water," said Frances. "I'll fluff up your pillows."

"Here's my summation," said Gloria. "You're living vicariously."

Frances picked up a pillow and hugged it. She needed a buffer. Gloria's cure might be harsher than Frances's condition.

"You're in love with an artist," said Gloria. "I have a pet theory. Women who hook up with artists have hidden agendas."

"I can take it," said Frances. She drew up her knees and embraced them.

"It's easier," said Gloria, "than being an artist themselves."

"I am not," answered Frances. "I'd be one by now. I'm too old."

"I could give you examples," said Gloria, "of famous late bloomers."

"I don't have a talent," said Frances.

"Maybe not," needled Gloria. "Take a lesson from Paul. He knows something about perseverance."

"I once kept a journal," said Frances. "I've tried to reread it. I don't like the person who wrote it. She didn't like people."

"That's the ticket," said Gloria. "Spare no one. Don't spare yourself either."

"Will I change if I write?" Frances asked. "Could it be I'm a monster?"

"Feed the monster," said Gloria. "It's your friend. It's your true inspiration. You should see the inside of my head if you're partial to monsters."

Frances went home. She had hoped to get answers, not prodding. She had hoped to hear Gloria lampoon the male sex, Paul included, making Paul very small, as she did with the men in her novels, like an impotent troll who attempted to hoodwink a witch. Frances counted the votes in her poll of Paul's actions and morals. One against; one abstaining. She wanted a clear-cut consensus. She groaned at the prospect of telling her story again. Perhaps she should write it and pass it around in a leaflet, or record it on tape, or wear it in sandwich-board fashion. When she collared Ruthanne, who was known for her vehement judgments, she mangled the narrative and had to repeat certain sections. "How old is the baby?" "No, no," Frances said. "It's not born yet." "You said it was black." "Not the baby; her previous lover." Ruthanne rubbed her eyes. She looked sullen as well as bewildered, as if her big sister had told her the crude facts of life. "This is over my head," said Ruthanne. "I'm too young. I don't get it."

One against; one abstaining; one psychically underaged voter. Since all else had failed, Frances stated the case to her mother. Eleanor Basinger, formerly Nelly Girard, was expecting her bridge club, which met every week on a Wednesday. "I can't chat for long," said her mother. "I'm ironing napkins." Frances gave her a shortened rendition, since Paul had once met Mrs. Basinger. She remembered him well, because Paul ate four helpings of capon, leaving nothing for lunch the next day but the wings and the carcass. As she spoke, Frances heard bursts of mist and the thunk of the iron. She heard a loud creaking: the ironing board being folded. Over the wires came more noises, a rattling and clinking. "Go on," said her mother. "I'm listening. I'm filling the nut cups." "I'll call back." Frances sighed. "You're distracted. I need your opinion." "I'm too old and too tired," said her mother. "I have no opinion."

In spite of the adage, confession is bad for the soul. It weakens the will and gives rise to undignified gossip. Frances might live to be ninety and rise to great heights: her confessors would never forget her involvement with scandal. Even now, there were signs she was tainted by the tale she had broadcast. Did people stop talking abruptly when Frances approached them? Why had Hammy walked right by her door without turning to hail her? Had Arlene, the receptionist, covered a laugh with her hand? There was only one person who saw Frances whole and unsullied. In the hour of her shame, only Gus was her aid and her comfort. His affection for Frances was balm to her dishonored spirit, and his feelings seemed warmer with each editorial session. Gus had no knowledge of Paul and his pact with the Devil; he did not look at Frances and see a discredited woman. The proofs for *The Sisterhood Murders* had come from the printer. Frances liked an excuse to flee Harwood and bold, prying glances, so she carried the galleys in person to Gus's apartment. Gus lived in a garden apartment, or, rather, a basement. The garden in question was paved with concrete cracked by frost heaves. The odd blade of grass struggled up through the breaks in the paving. A pile of old bricks and a birdbath were grouped in one corner. Artists often prefer to inhabit lugubrious dwellings, since cheerful surroundings distract them from higher endeavors. Gus's lodgings were Spartan and lacked any touches of color; the walls and the fabrics had aged to a mean shade of brown. The housekeeping habits of artists may also be careless; Gus's color scheme owed its appearance to layers of grime.

Gus welcomed Frances and pulled up two chairs to the table. She feared for the galleys as well as her sleeves and her cuffs. The top of the table bore traces of butter and egg yolk, a coating of cake crumbs and dust, and some splashes of tallow. Gus brought Frances hot tea in a mug that had once had a handle. As he gave her the cup, she observed that his neck was not clean. Outside his home, when he wore a starched shirt and a tie, she had never had reason to question his standards of grooming. Gus hovered near her, offering her sugar and milk. His shoulder brushed hers as he opened the package of galleys. As he studied the pages, she felt his hot breath on her cheek. His breath, to her boundless relief, was innocuous and sweet. If he pounced, she might yield to his kisses in spite of his neck. It was surely ungracious to fret about mere sanitation. Who was she, in her abject condition, to shun dirt and scurf?

If Gus had considered impinging on Frances's anatomy, he was quickly distracted by the sight of his work in cold print. He handled the pages as if they were made of blown glass, lip-reading certain fine phrases, or quoting aloud. Finding very few errors, he finished the proofs in short order. He thanked Frances profusely, and made her a fresh cup of tea. With his usual tact, he diverted the subject to Frances, showing earnest concern for his editor's health and well-being. Was she sleeping enough? he inquired. Was she working too late? Her pallor became her, but he feared it betokened fatigue. Gus's sympathy had the effect of a potent emetic. She could feel her sad squalid narration rise up in her gorge. She debated an instant before she released her confession, but Gus was her friend and she needed the male point of view.

Gus was her friend, but his face wore a queasy expression, as if she had made an unmentionable mess on the floor. Should she offer to fetch a wet mop and a bottle of ammonia? Should she open the windows to let out the stench of her story? Gus averted his eyes. Would he shrink if she tried to come near him? Writers ought to have stomachs for life with its grit and its cankers. Nothing human should alienate writers, nor priests, nor physicians.

"You must leave him," said Gus.

"We are living apart," answered Frances.

"You are tied to this man," Gus intoned. "You would like to excuse him."

"His work is important," said Frances.

"Bad men make bad art."

"He's not bad. He's intrepid."

"I can see that I've lost you," Gus said.

Gus turned aside, so that half of his face was in shadow. The look she had read as distaste was, in fact, one of sadness. There was no way to make reparation for wounding his feelings. She could hardly insult him by thanking him for his assistance. She could hardly explain that he, Gus, next to Paul, was a groundling; that Gus played it safe, whereas Paul battled life on the ramparts. She went to the door, but he made no attempt to detain her. She had lost a good friend and an author, as well as a suitor. Gus would take his next book to a house where he got a male editor, never knowing what part he had played in resolving her crisis.

Out on the street, Frances blinked and held on to the railing. The basement was dark and the impact of daylight was blinding. When her vision adapted, she saw things anew, in clear outline. Her interior vision had sharpened, as well as her eyesight. Like a patient whose fever has broken, she knew she was mending. She had won back the use of her mind, which was sick from wrong thinking. She had tried to fit Paul into frames that were cut for mere humans. She had judged him by standards established by average people. Worse than that, she had shrunk to their level by heeding their counsel. It was she, and not Paul, who was guilty of every betrayal.

Instead of returning to Harwood, she set out for home. Crowds gave way as she passed; lights turned green as she stepped off the curb. She hiked fifty-odd blocks at the rate of a mile in ten minutes. Her thoughts ran ahead of her feet, spanning years in short spaces. She prayed for occasions to prove her allegiance to Paul, such as lying on the witness stand or paying him visits in prison. With luck on her side, she could take any raps meant for Paul. She would serve out his sentence or swing from the noose as his proxy. If Paul predeceased her (by natural means, not juridical), she would keep the flame burning, as relics of Genius are bound to. She would spend her last years keeping would-be biographers guessing, and searching his papers to excise all trace of Kip Hillyer.

Instead of fatiguing her, walking made Frances feel stronger. This flush of new energy altered her view of the future. She had once met a Keeper of the Flame, a philosopher's widow, who spent every day cutting clippings from journals and newspapers. When an article mentioned her husband in critical terms, she wrote to its author, upbraiding him for his bad judgment. When a scholar applied for permission to quote her late husband, she denied it unless the book showered the great man with praise. As time passed and her husband was mentioned or quoted less often, the widow developed the symptoms of terminal illness. When his last book had gone out of print, she declined and died quickly. Such a prospect did not attract Frances. In fact, it repelled her. Certain men asked their mates to surrender their lives, but in general their wives volunteered. Paul demanded hard work and attention and depths of forbearance; he did not require meek acquiescence or blind immolation. No question that Paul took advantage; he needed close watching. She needed more watching than he did. She was apt to give in without fighting. A new contract with Paul would involve constant jockeying and haggling. They would barter and deal at a clamorous decibel level. Frances looked forward to the opening round of the contest. Had she wanted a placid romance, she would not have picked Paul.

The stairs to Paul's loft were lit dimly, like Gus Stafford's basement. As she climbed, she looked upward, in case there were suspect intruders. On the next-to-last landing the light bulb was flickering and dying, casting patterns of shadows, tall shapes that looked restless and sinister. She peered through the glimmer and walked with her back to the wall. The optics were tricky. One shadow was wearing a trench coat. Frances stopped in her tracks. This illusion was denser than shadow. It moved on long legs and it reached out long arms to restrain her. It was bearded but faceless. Its grasp was assured and familiar. Clutched to its bosom, she heard it address and enjoin her.

"Give me my keys," said the voice of her fate and her future.

"Never," vowed Frances. "I may not be big, but I'm fearless."

"We're going to get married," said Paul.

"Go ahead!" shouted Frances.

"Stop punching," he begged her. "We have to. It squares our accounts."

"I'll punch you," said Frances. "I like it. I'd like to punch her."

"Cut it out," ordered Paul. "There's no her. She's adopting a baby."

"When I'm finished with you," Frances warned, "I'll raise welts on the baby."

"We are going to get married," Paul said, "if I have to use chloroform."

She gave Paul a look like a dog with a stick in his jaws who is torn between two strong desires that are taxing his brain: holding on and maintaining control of his cherished possession, or releasing the stick in order to play with his master.

"You might be unfaithful," said Frances. "I'd never live through it."

"I won't be," Paul answered. "I promise. It makes too much trouble."

"I haven't agreed," Frances stalled. "There are certain conditions."

"Can't we settle this later?" asked Paul.

"Not so fast," answered Frances. "I need two more drawers in the bureau. And a shelf in the bookcase. And a desk of my own. And I want to retrieve my cat Lewis."

"Yes to everything!" Paul started growling.

"Your oath signed in blood," she continued. "No more improvs, ordeals, or experiments. No more Rudolf and Mary."

Paul was smiling, or baring his teeth, like a soreheaded lion.

"Watch your step," he advised, moving toward her. "Or I'll make you play Christians and Romans."

As a rule, brides-to-be who have just received marriage proposals do not pepper their probable lifemates with blows to the shoulders. The bridegroom-to-be, according to widespread tradition, does not pinion his fiancée's elbows and threaten to bite her. In most stories the outlaws are punished and rue their misdeeds. When the suicide play was performed for a live, paying audience, Paul was hailed as the boldest director of his generation. Many love stories end with a promise of ceaseless felicity. The prospects of Frances and Paul may inspire speculation. What mutations would each undergo in the course of their union? Would Paul ever learn to share milk products? Would Nip take possession of Frances? She hoped that he would: better Nip than the old wormy Frances. The new Frances Would cause some dismay in the ranks of her colleagues. Her family might never adjust to her picturesque habits. Paul himself would be forced to make frequent unselfish concessions, clearing space for her humors as well as her books, cat, and clothing. Someday Frances, not Paul, might need nursing through moods and obsessions. She might utter unnatural sounds when the fit was upon her, and assume twisted animal postures portraying frustration. How would Frances and Paul dwell in peace in the same legal household, unless their establishment boasted three floors and an annex? It is hard to imagine them eating their breakfast in silence, so attuned to each other that words rarely need to be spoken. Frances and Paul are not scheduled for marital concord. Two eccentrics who marry must live in a comradely uproar.

About the Author

ANN ARENSBERG was born in Pittsburgh, Pennsylvania, grew up in Havana, Cuba, and was educated at Radcliffe College and Harvard University. Short stories of hers have been included in the O. Henry Prize Stories Collections, and her novel, *Sister Wolf*, won the 1981 American Book Award for best first novel. She lives with her husband in New York City and Salisbury, Connecticut.

A Note on the Type

This book was set in a digitized version of Granjon, a type named in compliment to Robert Granjon, a type cutter and printer, active in Antwerp, Lyons, Rome, and Paris, from 1523 to 1590. Granjon, the boldest and most original designer of his time, was one of the first to practice the trade of type founder apart from that of printer.

Linotype Granjon was designed by George W. Jones, who based his drawings on a face used by Claude Garamond (ca. 1480–1561) in his beautiful French books. Granjon more closely resembles Garamond's own type than does any of the various modern faces that bear his name.

Composed by Adroit Graphic Composition Inc.,
New York, New York

Printed and bound by Fairfield Graphics,
Fairfield, Pennsylvania

Designed by Cecily Dunham

Arensberg, Ann
Group sex

(1) ✓✓✓

7day

JAN 23 87	DATE DUE		
APR 15 87			
JUN 2 87			
JAN 13 '88			
FEB 10 1988			
DEC 20 89			
JA 31 90			
APR 16 1991			
JAN 2 6 1993			